CUT TO THE CHASE

Praise for Lisa Girolami

Love on Location is… "An explosive and romantic story set in the world of movies."—*Diva Direct*

"The women of *Run to Me* are multi-dimensional and the running metaphor is well placed throughout this tale. Girolami has given us an entertaining story that makes us think—about relationships, about running away, and about what we want to run to in our lives."—*Just About Write*

Run to Me is… "An intense romantic story where love seems to be a lethal word."—*Diva Direct*

In *The Pleasure Set*… "Girolami has done a wonderful job portraying the wealthy dilettantes along with the complex characters of Laney and Sandrine. Her villain is a great combination of brains and ruthlessness. Of course, the sex scenes are fabulous. This novel is a great blend of sex, romance, and mystery, and the cover is perfect."—*Just About Write*

"[*Jane Doe*] is one of those quiet books that ends up getting under your skin. The story flowed with the ease of a slow-moving river. All in all a well-written story with an unusual setting, and well worth the read."—*Lambda Literary Foundation*

By the Author

Love on Location

Run to Me

The Pleasure Set

Jane Doe

Fugitives of Love

Cut to the Chase

CUT TO THE CHASE

by
Lisa Girolami

2013

CUT TO THE CHASE

ISBN 13: 978-1-60282-783-7

This Trade Paperback Original Is Published By
Bold Strokes Books, Inc.
P.O. Box 249
Valley Falls, NY 12185

First Edition: February 2013

CREDITS
EDITOR: SHELLEY THRASHER
PRODUCTION DESIGN: STACIA SEAMAN
COVER DESIGN BY SHERI (GRAPHICARTIST2020@HOTMAIL.COM)

Acknowledgments

My love and respect for Hollywood, the town that launched my career and whose stories I've lived and will remember forever.

A gracious nod to my buddy, Carsen Taite, who keeps me on the right side of the law.

Love and appreciation to Susan and all of her support.

Huzzah to Sheri and her mad cover skills.

Thank you to Shelley, the talented little bard that sits on my shoulder and draws red lines all over my ears.

And a howl out to Radclyffe, the best Alpha I could ever look up to.

To my Silver Girl.

CHAPTER ONE

I can do this, Avalon thought. She gripped the door's armrest as the wind rushed across her face.

"We're almost at sixty-five," the driver yelled, though her mind was so attuned to every sensation that a whisper would have sounded like thunder.

All she needed was to do it again, but this time, she was to hang out of the window of the sports car a little farther, reach around the front windshield, point over the hood, and fire off two rounds.

As she waited for her cue, streetlights and darkened storefronts raced past her like silent soldiers.

The much-too-eager grin plastered on her face had to go, so she bit her lip and grimaced, and the corners of her mouth dropped in pain.

"Sixty-five!"

Avalon's stomach jumped, which snagged a breath from her lungs. This was it. She lurched out the window and the windy assault blasted her eyes into a watery blur. The pavement below rushed by and she gritted her teeth so hard, she could have chipped a tooth. As piping-hot adrenaline shot through her body, she lifted up and over the windshield, focusing on a point over the hood to the left. In a split second, she fired once. Twice.

The radio resting in the driver's lap came to life. "Cut! I think we got the shot, Avalon!"

A whoosh of air passed by her ears as she slid back inside. She sat down hard on the leather seat and slapped the driver's knee.

"Whooo!" She tried to stretch her too-long legs in the cramped quarters of the sports car. Still high on adrenaline, she punched the stunt driver's arm.

"Owww," he said as he swerved from the blow.

He hit the gas, skidding into a U-turn in the middle of the street, and headed back to the director and camera crew. She looked out the window, watching the smear of colors that were buildings and neon signs.

At the top of her lungs, she yelled, "I could freakin' do this all night!"

❖

"Three out of five," Paige Cornish said as she took a step closer and pointed the gamer remote at the television. "I thought I could beat you at this stupid tennis game."

"Uh-uh. I won," Chris Bergstrom said. "You lost, fair and square. "I'm Billie Jean King, I'm Billie Jean King…" She raised her hands and danced around, watching the animated version of herself mimic her moves. Bending over, she patted the butt of her holey jeans, laughing hard as her twin did the same.

Paige sat down on the couch, tired from a rather difficult day of rearranging the furniture in her house in an attempt to erase three years of bad memories from her life. She scooted over so Chris could sit down. She'd been in her gym shorts and a rumpled yellow T-shirt all day. Just like the comfort food she'd had for lunch, which was a peanut-butter-and-jelly sandwich, these were her comfort clothes.

Chris had come over earlier to cheer her up. "Best friends aren't supposed to let their best friend lose," Paige said.

"You didn't." Chris smiled and put down the remote.

"Anyway, this isn't the way we should be spending a Friday night. My God, what have our lives come to?"

Paige pushed a sweaty lock of hair from her forehead. "What do you have in mind? Go to the bar and watch a bunch of lesbians get drunk and grind their hips into each other?"

Chris's expression was as flat as unleavened bread. It was probably a look she gave a fair share of the people she pulled over to ticket. Her short-cropped, thick head of brown hair, lightly dusted with gray, the no-nonsense olive-green eyes, and her strong, chiseled jawline completed the I'm-not-amused cop look. "Oh yeah, that'd be boring. Not to mention stupid. I mean, why would two single women even think of going out to meet some new people?"

"New drunk people."

"It's early. Most of them aren't drunk yet," Chris said as she pulled Paige's coffee table back over between the couch and television. "They look great."

"What?"

"Your books." Chris picked up Paige's newest release from the coffee table and leafed through it. It was a large-format book of bold and revealing photographs with text to match on each page. "*The End*. I love that title because it's so to the point. And the pictures are even better than the ones in your first one."

Chris handed the book to her and Paige turned *The End* over. She liked the author's picture on the back jacket. Her semi-curly brown hair usually behaved when she needed it to and had framed her eyes like a soft proscenium. She was glad to have worn a brown top that day because it complemented her blue eyes without making them look washed out. Her smile, however, was wider than she liked, but that was always the case.

"You think?"

Chris nodded to the other large-format book on the coffee table. "Don't misunderstand me. The shots you got with *Once Upon a Time* are classic. I know there are a lot of books out there about the movie business, but you've been able to write about and photograph it from way on the inside. The pictures on the movie sets are so candid and amazing. How are both of them selling?"

"*The End* is doing exceptionally well. But having two of the stars I featured in *The End* die right before it was released has helped make sales skyrocket."

"Strange coincidence. But it wasn't like you killed them yourself." Chris's stare was almost droll. "You have an alibi for those nights, right?"

"Coming from a cop, I guess that question shouldn't surprise me."

Chris shrugged. "Well, sales are sales. I mean, what can you do?"

"Nothing, I suppose."

"There is something, Miss Bestselling Author. We can go to the bar and let your fans maul you."

"Hardly bestselling."

"You told me yourself that you're getting fan mail just because of your picture on the jacket cover." She pinched Paige's cheek. "You shouldn't be stingy with the public."

Paige batted her hand away. "Can't we just go get a pizza or something?"

Eyeing her as she would if she'd just pulled her over for speeding, Chris said, "You're afraid Marlene will be there, aren't you?"

A surge of trepidation rose quickly, filling Paige's stomach and throat with dread. "No."

"Come on, it could be fun. We're just two hapless gals, recently dumped by our exes and looking for love."

"Speak for yourself. I'm not hapless. Just…unfortunate."

"Let's get out of the house." Her whine grated, which was the objective.

"Do you really want to go? Fine, I'll go with you. But don't expect me to be the life of the party."

Chris got up and held her hand out. Paige let herself be pulled up and sighed as she acquiesced to what might be a trip to Regretsville.

Groaning from the dead weight, Chris said, "I just expect my best friend to hang out with me and have a beer and a laugh."

"And if I don't laugh?"

Chris pulled her pants leg up to reveal an ankle holster. "Then I'll just shoot you."

"Okay, Officer Bergstrom. But you're driving."

❖

"That's Avalon Randolph," one of two teenagers said behind her.

Avalon had stopped by a Starbucks to grab a double espresso. She knew they'd have lots of coffee on the movie set, but she was jonesing for a freshly pulled espresso.

She tried to ignore the conversation behind her but couldn't help hearing bits of the dialogue. "She's gorgeous!" "Should I ask her for an autograph?" "She doesn't look like a party girl."

Avalon ordered and paid and then made her way to the pick-up end of the coffee bar. She'd heard that this particular Starbucks was the best place to be left alone. It was secluded in an upscale neighborhood off Beverly Glen and Mulholland, and most people looked like they were from the neighborhood. A few over-Botoxed middle-aged women and the usual smattering of wannabe screenwriters sat tapping away on their laptops. The baristas were all attractive in the way that suggested they were only working at that location so they could get connections for a job in entertainment.

Sure enough, an exchange between two seated customers close by confirmed her observation.

"Any forward motion on that script you showed me last year?"

"Yeah. I think it's getting hot. It's at Ben Stiller's office but

I haven't heard back. And my Pilates instructor is going to see if Seth McFarlane wants to read it!"

"Wow. Seth McFarlane."

The two teenagers must have ordered because they were now standing right beside her. What came next was the uncomfortable silence that preceded some giggles and then hurried whispers. Avalon wasn't a neophyte at this routine, but it never became any less awkward.

"Excuse me?" one of the girls said. She sounded as meek as a virgin bride.

Avalon turned and smiled. She knew what was next.

"May I have your autograph?"

"Of course," Avalon said as the teenager thrust a pen and Starbucks nutrition guide at her.

"What's your name?"

"It's Paula, and I love your films! I've seen every one! And you look beautiful in person! I told my friend, Valerie, here, that you would be nice and you are!"

Valerie joined in and they were talking at the same time. "I knew she'd be nice. You can tell by the roles she plays."

"We can't wait for your next movie, but I got everything else on DVD. I'm keeping them forevs! And I saw your interview about the movie you're shooting now. It looks so cool!"

Avalon could tell that others around them were looking up from their drinks and conversations. A few cell phones came out of purses and pockets. She wrote a quick note and signed her name. The excited girls were still talking when she handed it back.

"I graduate from high school this May," Paula said, "and I want to start acting. I should go to college and maybe I'll go to film school, but my parents want me to study economics or something like that."

One of the attractive baristas handed Avalon the espresso.

"No matter what college you choose, just get a good education," she said.

As she walked away, she counted to four and, perfectly on cue, an eruption of giggles came.

Most of her actor friends not only loved the attention but sought it out. They'd walk up and down Melrose, drinking in the ardor and fervor of the public as if it were the Mojave Desert getting a long-awaited rainfall. Avalon would rather keep to herself more than not, but true moments of privacy were now scarce. And given the choice between awkward fan encounters and a paparazzi blitz, she'd take signing autographs for enthusiastic girls any day.

Plus, those teenagers were rather cute in their excitement, and she was grateful for their admiration. It hadn't been that long ago that she would have acted the same way around a celebrity.

❖

Paige and Chris sat on bar stools that looked out over the Lucky Strike bowling lanes. Though it was normally a heterosexual hangout, many Hollywood businesses included homosexual nights on their schedule since a buck was, in fact, a buck. So the third Friday of each month was lesbian bowling night. The place was crowded and Paige sipped her whiskey sour as she watched the playful bowlers fist pump and laugh at their varied athletic skills.

The ultra-plush contemporary décor would seem out of place given the retro shabbiness of the bowling lanes, but state-of-the-art lighting and fantastic music made it all come together nicely.

Paige had to admit that it was nice to get out of her apartment. She'd deliberately stayed away from bars and other nighttime activities to avoid running into her ex. But tonight, she felt a little stronger. The humiliation of being cheated on still simmered like a pot of thick, stewing soup, but the level was low now, just a roiling of crusty yuckiness clinging to the bottom.

The women at Lucky Strike were as diverse as Los Angeles, white, Latina, black, and Asian women mingled with jovial spirits. Everyone seemed to be having a good time, and none of the typical incidents of arm-waving, drunken drama were erupting from the crowd.

She checked her watch. Of course, it was still early.

"What do you think of those two?" Chris pointed her half-full shot glass toward lane number four.

Of the four women bowling, two were obviously together because they had their arms wrapped tight around each other. The other two were probably in their early thirties, and their relaxed, casual body language made them appear to be pals. One was tall with red hair and accessories so bohemian that Paige speculated she might be a poet. The other, an Asian woman, appeared to be a swimmer or volleyball player, judging by the definition of her shoulders. The women were dressed almost exactly alike in black pants and yellow tops.

"The ones that look like twins? I don't know."

"I think they'd like to have drinks sent over."

"Meaning you want to hook up with one of them?"

"Well, maybe."

Paige groaned out loud. "Can't we just hang out and watch the supremely amusing sportiness of all these women heaving twelve-pound balls down the lane?"

"You need to get back on the horse, my friend."

"My last horse had a fit of bucking and threw me into the dirt. I'm not sure my ass has recovered from the impact."

"Can you tell what they're drinking?"

"Chris, if you send drinks over, then we'll have to talk to them."

"That's the point, ding-dong."

A cocktail waitress plopped a shot of whiskey down in front of Chris. "This is for you."

Paige raised her eyebrows. "That was fast."

"Who's it from?" Chris said.

The waitress jerked her head to her left. "Behind you. The woman in the white tank top."

Paige and Chris turned around. Standing at the pool table, a fairly feminine woman with long blond hair raised her bottle of beer.

As the waitress walked away, Chris looked at Paige and grinned.

"Go on," Paige told her.

"I don't want to leave you here."

"I'm fine. Just let me know if I need a ride home."

Chris began to get up but hesitated. "No. I'm not leaving my buddy."

"The twins are on frame seven and they're neck and neck. I have to see how this game turns out."

Chris smirked, knowing Paige was full of it.

Paige pushed her shoulder. "Go, already."

Chris left and Paige raised her own glass of whiskey. She downed the rest of it, wincing at the potent, burnt-oak aftertaste.

She was single again, and that was okay with her. Sure, she'd like to meet someone nice, someone who wanted the same things she did. Marlene was now her ex. That sounded so weird. She really hadn't ever thought their relationship would end. Especially in the deceitful way that it had. She thought they wanted the same things. And she thought they could work through anything. But obviously Marlene had a different opinion.

She waved to the cocktail waitress and felt the thick molasses of sadness coating her heart. It would eventually pass, she knew, but for now, she wouldn't pursue any new relationships. She had to put together her thoughts on the next book. Writing and photography would be the twins she'd be dating for a while. They wouldn't keep her warm at night, but neither had Marlene toward the end. And work couldn't hurt you.

CHAPTER TWO

I t's a go."
Paige listened to those big words coming through her small cell phone. She hadn't expected the news so quickly, but then again, she hadn't expected the extraordinary sales figures on her last book. "Go, as in start now?"

Carmen Garza, her publisher, minced few words. "Go as in yesterday. I'll expect a draft in three months."

"Three months?" Panic rose in her throat. It had taken a year to complete her last book.

"It's called momentum, darling."

She hung up and stared at her last two books. They had been exciting to produce, but the hours of photographing the actors and actresses, all on the go as they worked, plus the long nights of writing about each experience, had been an arduous undertaking.

Her first pictorial book, *Once Upon a Time*, told the behind-the-scenes stories of shooting romantic films. She'd gained access to actors and actresses while they were on set or on location and had photographed them as the crew filmed the scenes. Then she'd sat with the actors and more or less interviewed them. It became more or less because most interviews started out with a specific direction and formal questions but quickly went off page and ran the gamut from silliness to bitch sessions to very personal disclosures.

For *The End*, her second book, she took the same approach while documenting the filming of movie endings. She knew she'd struck upon a great formula but wasn't quite sure what it was. Sometimes she felt like a therapist who just listened to her subjects. She could sense when they had something else to say and would encourage them to expound. It might be a certain look or a word they uttered that might normally go unnoticed, but Paige was always so connected with her interviewees that they must have felt her curiosity and empathy. Hilarious anecdotes and very private thoughts filled her pages, and, coupled with the powerful photographs she was blessed to capture, they had become a successful venture.

This time, her book would be called *Cut to the Chase* and she would follow the films that had action scenes. She needed to start her homework, scanning industry periodicals and making phone calls to create a list of the current movies being produced that fit the bill. With the help of the producers whom she'd had contact with from her last books, she would be able to visit the sets she needed and get going.

But all of this in three months? How would she be able to pull that off?

She had to conduct research on what movies would be appropriate for her topic, write and rewrite outlines, call managers and agents, arrange interviews, cull through thousands of images, and spend countless hours at the computer to clean up the photographs. Of course, many times actors would cancel appointments, and then the waiting game would commence. And then she'd have to endure the editing process and reviews with her publisher that would send her back to rewrite text or reassemble photo layouts.

The image of a rising waterline came to mind. Even if she somehow floated up with it, her nostrils might fill and the deluge would overcome her. She knew she didn't need to, but she took a deep breath and held it.

❖

Three hours and four cups of coffee later, Paige had copies of *Variety* and *Hollywood Reporter* spread out on her table, along with *Back Stage* and dozens of pieces of paper with notes of her phone calls to everyone she knew. She sighed heavily. One final call to the Screen Actors Guild had supplied her with useful information. When asking about working stuntmen, she was told that two films listed themselves as action movies. One starred Bubba Densman, a surly stuntman turned actor, and the other featured Ricky Boswell, an actor who wouldn't do his own stunts, no matter how simple. Only two films. This wasn't good news. She needed to include actresses as well, since she didn't want the book to be unbalanced. Angelina wasn't currently working and Demi was busy producing. Who could she find?

Looking out her front window, she listened as the garden fountain in her complex splashed and gurgled happily like the musings of a little toddler who thinks no one is watching. She loved her apartment, located in a historic area of West Hollywood, which provided her with lots of plants, sunlight, and quiet. It was smaller than most other places she'd considered when she'd looked years before, but it preserved the elegance of old Hollywood to perfection. Plus, other than a bed, bathroom, and kitchen, all she needed was a place to write and edit photographs on her laptop.

She reviewed her notes, scanning them for anything she'd missed. Nothing there.

Then she picked up the phone.

"Phil? It's Paige Cornish."

"Paige! How are you? Thank you for the plug you gave my last film in your book. Great work!" Phil Cornwell had generously given her carte blanche to one of the movies she'd covered. They'd developed a nice friendship and she'd sent him a thank-you copy of *The End* when it was first published.

"Thanks. It helped that you produced a blockbuster."

"Thanks back at you. Your books are selling well, I hear."

"They are."

"What can I do for you?"

"Bubba Densman is shooting an action film. Who else is starring?"

"No big names."

"The Ricky Boswell film is the only other action film I found. Any more that you know of?"

"Yeah. Brent Hastings is shooting around LA. It's not technically an action film like Bubba's, but it does have some pretty intense moments. And I hear he's doing his own stunts."

"Really?"

"Yeah. It's Birney Phillips's film. They're not yet hitting the PR folks that heavily yet. Don't know why."

"Problems with the filming?"

"Nah. Probably just a marketing position. I'd guess it's because Avalon Randolph is opposite Brent."

"Avalon Randolph? As a romantic lead?"

Phil laughed. "No. You'd think so. She's playing his nemesis."

"She's a comedic actress."

"She is, but I hear she's got some great action chops."

"Really?"

"You want Birney's number? I can call ahead and tell him to give you free rein."

"That would be fantastic. Thank you!"

She hung up the phone and her heart began to pump harder than if she'd had four more cups of coffee.

If she were ever forced to admit a fantasy crush, it would be on Avalon Randolph. Of course, she had to share that crush with about six million other people. Never mind that Avalon was known for her brash behavior and sharp tongue; she was Hollywood's darling, with a popular TV series and an impressive string of five successful romantic-comedy movies under her gold-filled Gucci belt. She was the favorite cover girl of Hollywood celebrity magazines and featured on most entertainment news shows fairly often.

Everyone knew that Avalon was hot and beautiful and very funny, but it wasn't common knowledge yet that she was branching out into action movies. And playing a nemesis, no less.

Paige drummed her fingers on the table as her excitement quickly rose. What a coup it would be if she could get Avalon in her book. It would really help publicize it, not to mention boost sales. And spotlighting Avalon on the cover instead of Bubba or Ricky would make her day.

Hell—she stopped and took a deep breath—who was she kidding? Just meeting her would make her day.

❖

The sun gently warmed Avalon's face as she laid her head back on the convertible's seat rest. The wind mussed her hair, pulling tendrils back as if almost massaging her head. Avalon was in the passenger's seat, next to Leah, who was driving. Ivy and Sandy sat in the back. They were all actresses who had remained casual friends over the last few years and got together when they could.

As Leah's BMW sped north on the Pacific Coast Highway, Avalon closed her eyes and let the cool, brackish smell of the ocean fill her lungs. They were heading to Bui Sushi in the Malibu Colony, and when Leah turned off PCH and onto Malibu Road, Avalon opened her eyes and lifted her head. They left the rocky cliffs to the north and entered an area of tightly knit homes and businesses, all staking their ocean-view claims as if they were concertgoers elbowing each other in front of the stage.

Sunday was Avalon's only day off on the six-day shooting schedule that the producers of her movie had contracted her to do. She had some free days when she wasn't in a scene to be shot, but since she was playing the lead role, they were as scarce as chaste casting couches.

They reached Bui Sushi and were led to a table by the sushi bar. The dark wood walls and décor offered a nice and welcoming contrast to the brightly lit day outside.

Ivy always ordered for them all, and soon a number of appetizers were dispensed to their table.

"Who's going to Cannes this year?" Leah asked as they all helped themselves to the edamame, tuna tartare on wonton chips, shrimp-and-veggie tempura, and spicy scallop rolls. She'd established her career in independent films and had stayed there, opting for more creative control, she often said.

"I go every year," Sandy, the tallest of the group, replied.

"Every year?" Avalon couldn't see the reason. Sure, if she were a producer or director, the Cannes Film Festival would be a great place to promote a film. But mostly, it consisted of a lot of rather formal and very restrained cocktail parties and starched screenings for the judges.

"Sure," Sandy said. "See and be seen, you know?"

The waiter refilled their glasses of water and Avalon almost asked for a Coca-Cola, but didn't want to fend off the raised eyebrows and snorts she'd get about the constant battle to remain a size zero. For some reason, she always behaved a little differently around these friends. They never drank anything but water at meals and ordered the lowest-calorie plate on the menu, then ate only half. She was sure at least Leah was bulimic, and probably Sandy and Ivy, so part of her didn't want to gorge in front of them and part caved into the Tinseltown tenet that starving oneself meant more opportunities for work. Even though it would be refreshing and comforting, ordering a sugary drink was tantamount to going off the deep end. She sighed as the waiter poured the water.

"Plus, the deal-making is spectacular," Leah said. "At the small restaurant tables down at the beach, you can almost smell the money shifting hands."

"Speaking of that," Ivy crunched on some edamame, "you know that place on Carbon Beach, close to the Malibu Pier?" She jerked her head toward the restaurant's front door. "The one that's called Deal Maker's Rock?"

"That's supposedly where studio bosses and agents exercise in the morning while talking shop," Sandy said.

Ivy nodded. "Not supposedly. That's where my agent got my last film."

"Serious?" Sandy looked doubtful.

"That's what he said."

Avalon played with her rainbow roll. She didn't feel like engaging in the conversation. She'd almost wished Leah had kept driving up the coast, to nowhere in particular, because the whooshing of the wind had made her feel very nearly happy.

Why was she so mellow? She was starring in a spectacular motion picture, was finally free of her nasty girlfriend, and life couldn't be better. She looked around the table.

Ivy was at the top of her game in comedic rolls that just kept coming. Sandy had scored big, playing the lead in a superhero film that had made her high kicks a fantasy of teenagers around the world. And Leah couldn't go anywhere without her indie following and tweeting her every move.

While the four of them often went to lunch or shopped on Melrose Avenue, she couldn't actually say that any of these women were her close friends. More than anything, they'd thrown themselves together because of their work. It was easier to hang out with other actresses because of the unspoken oath of confidentiality among them. They all understood what problems could arise from the verbal spillings of a well-meaning but overly excited, non-industry acquaintance.

They had a lot of fun when they were together, but honestly, Avalon doubted she could call any of them in the middle of an emotionally bad night.

So why did she keep hanging out with them? Maybe a better question was, who was she closer to that she could hang out with? Her ex had been the one lately, but now that they had split, Avalon hadn't found much in the way of consistency. That is, except for the reliable bars she was frequenting more often and the unfailing paparazzi that seemed to always be around.

She felt as if she were in a bubble, with her work, her agent and manager, and her fellow sushi-eating comrades forming the shell inside which she dwelled. The paparazzi were the sharp pins that persistently threatened to burst the bubble. And if they did, she wasn't sure there would be any substance and meaning in what they found.

Leah, Sandy, and Ivy were deep into a conversation about luxury resorts, and Avalon turned away from them to look around the room.

Couples were huddled close and families with children were animated in their interactions. They were all ordering food and laughing and talking as if their meal was just another wonderful pearl in the content and happy necklace of their lives. A flash of metal or something outside made her focus on the restaurant's front window.

As the waiter came around to check on her table, Avalon recognized the unrelenting and scheming body language of a fistful of scruffy, camera-toting men hovering around the entrance.

Ah, hell, she thought as she turned back to the table and, specifically, the waiter. "Would you please bring me a Coke?"

CHAPTER THREE

A rather large group of Avalon's fans was pushing and pressing into each other to get closer to her. She wanted to shake some hands, but she had on expensive cream-colored pants and a matching sleek jacket that the wardrobe department had just given her to wear for the next scene. She couldn't afford to get them dirty; if she did, the director and crew would have to wait for them to be cleaned by hand.

The movie set's security kept the crowd at bay, but Avalon reached around the guards to carefully sign as many autographs as she could.

"I love you," one male fan in all-black leather called out.

"I love you, too," she replied, tremendously energized by the adoration. This was evidence that she was a star. She was on top and riding the wave like a professional surfer, and the crowd worshipped her as she shredded the waves of Hollywood.

She relished her celebrity, knowing that there was nothing more powerful than the current status quo of the mighty triple play: fame, money, and fan worship.

"Time to go, Miss Randolph." One of the security guards motioned toward the set. Reluctantly, she waved good-bye to everyone and was whisked off.

The schedule for the day had the film crew on La Cienega Boulevard shooting a scene between Avalon and Brent Hastings.

Her agent, Billy Woods, had stopped by as she was finishing

up in the makeup trailer. Somebody named Paige Cornish wanted to interview her and shoot some pictures of her action scenes for a book she was writing. The always-hyper Billy said it would be good publicity.

"No one reads books," she said, nodding to Helen, her personal assistant, when she handed her a latte. Well-organized and solicitous, Helen Yang was a firecracker of a woman with impossibly long and thick black hair that was constantly tied back as if being disciplined. She always wore something efficient, like the black slacks and a tight white shirt she had on that day, probably because she had no time to mess about with frills.

"It's one of those pictorial coffee-table books," Billy said. "Her first two are doing very well and there's a lot of PR around them."

"This and about forty TV interviews before this movie gets done, Billy."

"Would I ask you if I didn't think it would be good for you?"

"Ahhh!" she bellowed. "It'll be a pain in the ass."

"But it's a pain in a good kind of ass."

The latte was perfect. The warmth flowed down her throat and settled in her stomach like a welcomed friend. She knew she shouldn't have caffeine; everyone always reminded her that she was naturally overly energetic, but she drank caffeinated drinks partly because people didn't want her to.

She looked at Billy before she took another sip. Sometimes she wondered if he ate every day. He rarely touched his food when they were at business lunches. He couldn't be more than one hundred and ten pounds, which had to be judiciously spread out over his five-foot-ten frame. His slender shoulders and arms connected to a skeletal torso that attached to his scrawny legs like a marionette held together by string. It didn't help that he wore tight sports coats and skinny pants, but considering that he was constantly in a nervous fidget, he didn't need to be concerned with gaining any weight. And just like her sometime lunch friends, Billy succumbed to the emaciated-is-essential expectations of Hollywood. That kind of treacherous propaganda skewed people's self-perception and cruelly whispered, "You're not perfect enough," into the ears of anyone with damaged self-esteem.

"Plus, TV shows come and go. A book stays around forever."

Narrowing her eyes at him, she said, "In the future when I tell you no, remember that I said yes to this one."

❖

Paige drove up to Chris Bergstrom's driveway just as Chris's police cruiser pulled in. The black-and-white was emblazoned with decals of a German shepherd and the letters *K9* on the sides.

"Perfect timing," Chris said as she let a beautiful German shepherd out of the backseat of her car. His short fawn coat with its black, dusky overlay of fur and black police harness made him look distinguished and ready for business, but it was the distinctively acute pricked-up ears and dark eyes that truly revealed his keen expression and serious intelligence.

"Hey, Abel!" Paige greeted the dog, who came over to sniff her.

"Sit," Chris said in Dutch, and the dog immediately sat.

"Abel is bilingual. He's smarter than me."

"And he behaves better."

"I picked up steaks." Paige held up a grocery bag.

As Chris grilled in the backyard, Paige brought out two bottles of beer and handed one to her as she sat at the patio table next to the grill. The yard was overgrown, like those of most of the well-established homes in the neighborhood. Tall, thick trees encompassed the fence line, providing shade for most of the day. A fairly good-size area of grass, lined with a brick walkway, allowed Abel to get some exercise, although he had to be careful of the flower bed that ran along the east side. The slats of the wood awning that covered the patio let in stripes of warm sunshine.

"I just found out I have three months to finish this next book," Paige said. "It's about action movies."

"Isn't that a bit tight?"

"Yeah. But I had to salute smartly and agree," she said, watching Abel chew on a rubber ball. "Only three movies are shooting right now that have the scenes I need."

"That won't fill a book."

"No, but I have a plan."

Abel picked up the ball and walked over to her. Dropping it at her feet, he sat down, his eyes alert as he watched her every move, obviously hoping for a game of fetch. She picked the ball up, feigned a throw to the right, and then threw it to the left. With whip-cracking speed, Abel charged after it.

"I can go much further in depth and dissect the action scenes from start to finish. I can document how they're planned, rehearsed, and shot. And I can write about all the different camera angles. That way, I can get a book's worth from only three films."

"That sounds interesting. I bet people will get a kick out of seeing how moviemakers put everything together."

Abel returned with the ball and lay down in front of Paige, chewing the ball and eyeing her. "There's something else people might get a kick out of."

Chris took a sip of her beer. "What?"

Abel dropped the ball and tapped it with his nose. It rolled toward Paige and she threw it again.

"One of the actors is Avalon Randolph."

Chris fumbled with the BBQ fork, almost dropping it. "Wild woman Avalon Randolph? Shit, are you kidding me?"

She shook her head.

"Doing an action film?"

Abel returned and Paige pitched the ball again. "Yup."

Chris stared at her. "Avalon Randolph?"

"You already said that." But she had said the same thing over and over, too.

"Oh my God. That's unbelievable."

"What's unbelievable is that you're about to burn our dinner."

Chris turned toward the blazing steaks and quickly moved them away from the flames. "And you're going to interview her?"

"That's the plan."

"Is the plan also to charm her into a date?"

Paige laughed. No way would an actress of that caliber be interested in her. Plus, she could never handle someone with such an uncontrollable personality. "Of course not."

Abel was back at Paige's feet, whining for another throw. She picked up the ball and tossed it again.

Abel snagged the ball in one bounce and Chris said, "It could happen."

No, it couldn't, she thought. That was like a third-grader thinking she'd marry her teacher. Different worlds. Different galaxies, actually. "I'll have a hard enough time just interviewing her."

Chris took a swig of her beer. "Man. That's incredible. You're going to hang out with her. She's, like, the biggest thing in Hollywood. She's a superstar."

"You're making me even more nervous, Chris."

"Hell. She's single. At least that's what the magazines say. And you're single. Why not?"

"Why, is more like it. She can have anyone she wants. Male or female."

"But she likes females, Paige. And you're one."

"That's about my only matching prerequisite. I'm not beautiful, rich, or famous."

"Who says those are the only qualities she's looking for? And besides, you are beautiful."

"We're not going to have this conversation. I am not looking to hook up. I'm writing a book."

"You'll win her over with your charms," Chris said. "Now hand me those plates and let's eat."

Paige stood and ruffled the fur on Abel's head. She wasn't too sure she could. She'd be meeting Avalon the next day and already her stomach was doing a river dance.

CHAPTER FOUR

"Cut!" The director called to the crew and they began to set up for the next scene. Avalon made her way to the corner of Hollywood Boulevard and Vine Street and stepped out of the hot June sun and into the makeup trailer.

Tawnya, her personal hair and makeup woman, was also her best friend. A tall, beautiful black woman, Tawnya wore lots of red and black. Whether she chose formal wear or jeans and a T-shirt, she always looked incredibly stylish. When she had done an outstanding job on Avalon's first film, Avalon had asked for her on each succeeding film. She trusted her not only with her hair and makeup but also her secrets.

"It's a bit sticky out there." She opened a bottle of water just as she heard a knock at the door.

"Come in," Tawnya said as she blotted the sweat from Avalon's face.

She turned to see a rather stunning woman step in. Dressed in shapely jeans and a white V-neck T-shirt, the woman looked like an actress, but Avalon didn't recognize her from the set. Her long brown hair looked to curl naturally as it fell about her shoulders. Avalon could see the beautiful cerulean blue of her eyes even from that distance. She had a big, wide smile that made Avalon's stomach flutter.

"I'm Paige Cornish," she said, holding out a business card.

Her pleasant, almost deferential manner had a refreshing appeal. "I'm here to interview you."

"The writer." She took the card. At first, she'd balked at Billy's request for this interview. Sure, it was part of her job, but the constant barrage of the same questions and the same requests for poses had become tedious and mind-numbing. Paige, however, seemed to lack the typical assertive approach of a reporter or writer. Avalon could always sense the ulterior motives of an interviewer by the way the air around them smelled of anxious career-climbing and scoop-grabbing. Their mouths usually crooked up in covetousness, as if they were going to suck the soul right out of her and pawn it for a buck or two.

Paige's face didn't show any of that. Her eyes were bright, not with greed but with thoughtfulness. She seemed void of the nastiness of entertainment reporting.

This might be more enjoyable than Avalon had imagined.

Paige stepped over and offered her hand. She took it. "So you're going to follow me around and write about…what?"

Paige opened the satchel she was carrying and handed her a rather large book. "Here's a copy of my last one. It'll give you an idea of what I do."

"*The End*, a study of movie endings." She flipped through the coffee-table-size tome, immediately impressed with the photographs. Some were in color and others in black and white, but they all looked remarkable in their composition. Avalon didn't know a lot about photography, but she'd picked up enough working with cinematographers.

One once told her that the subject matter, meaning the actors, weren't always the most important thing. He looked at each scene as an arrangement of light and dark and of colors and shapes.

Paige understood what he was saying. Her use of bold, broad elements and strong lines was exactly what made her images so powerful.

Avalon flipped through the candid images and prepared

setups, and the subjects, most of whom Avalon knew, seemed so real and alive they appeared to jump off the page.

The motor-home door opened and the second assistant director stepped in. "*Entertainment Tonight* is here, Avalon. They said they have an interview with you."

She read the text that accompanied a shot of a costar she'd worked with, captivated by the way Paige had described the scene and analyzed the significance of its simple directness.

"Avalon?"

She held her hand up as she finished reading the text.

Looking at Paige she said, "This is really good."

Helen came in and stood behind the second assistant director. "Avalon, Charles Herrera called again about the clothing line he's designing. He wants to have dinner with you."

"And this is your second book?"

Paige nodded. "It is. The one I'm working on now is called *Cut to the Chase*."

"Action scenes."

"Yes."

The second assistant director and Helen said simultaneously, "Avalon?"

She sighed before turning away from Paige. "Tell *Entertainment Tonight* that I'll get to them when I can. And schedule Charles for sometime next month. Or later." As they left, she said to Paige, "Well, I'm a newbie at this action genre, but I'll do my best."

Avalon turned back to face the mirror and Tawnya began to touch up her mascara. "Avalon's already got the whole crew on their toes."

"I'm sorry." Avalon held out her hand, palm up. "This is Tawnya."

"Nice to meet you," Paige said. "Would it be possible to interview you as well?"

Tawnya laughed. "You do know how dangerous that is, don't you?"

Avalon could see from the reflection in the mirror that Paige's raised eyebrows revealed that she didn't.

"You mean because you're my personal hair and makeup person," Avalon said, "or because you're my best friend?"

"Either." Tawnya picked up some blush and began to apply it under Avalon's cheeks. "I don't get paid to do hair and makeup. I get paid to shut up."

"That's not true." She slapped Tawnya's arm before turning to Paige. "She can say anything she wants. My life is an open book. For your book."

Tawnya rolled her eyes. "Witty."

"Am I done, Tawnya? I've got an interview to do." She looked at Paige and was suddenly taken with the prettiest wide-mouthed smile she'd ever seen. If there was a picture to go with the term *winning smile*, it was Paige's.

Paige walked with Avalon to the set of *The Last Stand*, which, today, was located at the corner of Sunset and Vine. She was used to being on movie sets and, having interviewed a fair number of celebrities, had learned much about how they were organized. But this time, she felt so nervous she was afraid she'd trip or bump into someone as they walked. The first time she'd seen Avalon in a movie theater, she'd been hooked by her striking beauty. She was probably five foot nine, not extremely tall for an actress, but so perfectly shaped, she could have chosen a career in athletics. She seemed naturally strong, with legs and arms that were noticeably well formed. And on more than one occasion, Paige had shamelessly stared at her ass on the big screen, wondering how perfection like that was possible. What made her even more attractive to Paige was that her roles usually depicted her as smart, straightforward, and capable, with a propensity toward clever wisecracks and adorable repartee.

Off camera, she was known to be rowdy and not inclined to follow rules. She seemed to have nothing but fun, and Hollywood made sure to cover practically every moment. It seemed that almost every night, TV shows would regale her with Avalon's antics at Hollywood bars, Melrose clothing stores, or movie premieres. But what Paige knew about her was only what she'd seen and read. Was she really as boisterous as they reported, as well as slightly out of control? Nothing written ever mentioned any specific diva moments, but with her level of celebrity status, wasn't that part of the expected behavior?

As they walked, Paige scrutinized Avalon. She wore a tailored gray pantsuit and a black blouse, looking like the stylish but expert detective she was portraying. As she watched her walk with the confidence of a lioness in the midst of her pride, a lot of great adjectives circulated through her head and Paige mentally wrote text for her book: self-assured, poised, fearless, jaunty, cocky. But who was Avalon, the person?

A jolt of reality zipped through her. She was actually *hanging out* with Avalon Randolph. Would she get to see the other side of the actress, the part of her life that was truly her and not what every public camera captured? Would she be shy and reserved, the antithesis of most of her on-screen characters? Would she be an obsessive-compulsive hairball, creating a maelstrom of anxiety and tension for those around her? What was she like to just sit and talk to? Who did she admire? What did she think of Hollywood as a business? Paige had so many questions she hoped Avalon would answer.

There seemed to be no question, however, of her sexual preference. She was an out lesbian and her past girlfriends were well documented in magazines and on entertainment shows. Her last was Jessica Wiley, another famous celebrity who commanded almost as much per movie as some research had revealed that Avalon was supposedly getting for her first action film.

It was fairly hot out and the sun bore down on them as they

walked down Vine. Avalon sauntered along, but there was a paradoxical purposefulness in the way she did. The combination was an alluring trick, like she was convincing you that she was relaxed but was ready, in a heartbeat, to react with speed and precision.

As soon as they neared the crew and cameras, they ducked under a large shade cover. Avalon's director's chair was there, along with a number of others. Avalon motioned for her to sit next to her. "So, tell me, how does this work?"

She sat down, placing the satchel in her lap. "It's a longer process than usual. I photograph the action scenes you're in and we talk in between. Or, if it's easier for you, we can arrange one longer interview session instead."

"Let's just see how it goes."

"That's fine."

"I liked the book you showed me. It's really unique."

"Thank you."

"I hope I can give you some good shots."

"I'm sure you will," Paige said. "When's your next action scene?"

"This afternoon. It's a small one, a short fight, but you might like it."

"Great. I'll be taking pictures before and during the camera work. After, too." Paige cringed and hoped that the sudden upturn of the corner of her mouth was the only telltale sign. It was obvious that taking pictures afterward was included in what she'd be doing. Sheesh!

Avalon smoothed over a section of her pants leg but Paige hadn't noticed a wrinkle.

"Do I get to see the photographs?"

"Sure," Paige said. "All of them, if you like."

"So, how do you like working on and around movie sets?"

"It's better than taking high school yearbook pictures."

Avalon laughed out loud, which surprised Paige. Of course,

she'd chosen that answer to be witty, but Avalon's reaction had seemed so genuine and cordial that it flustered her for a moment.

"Did you used to do that?"

"Actually, I did. It was a way to make money to finish college."

"I bet you saw a lot."

Paige shrugged. "A lot of pranksters and goofballs. It seems that a lot of kids would rather not be memorialized for their studies but for their shenanigans."

"Sounds like an assembly-line nightmare."

"Yes, but it paid the bills."

"And now your books pay the bills?"

"They're starting to. I also sell photos to websites and things like that. But, yes, I was able to walk away from yearbook hell."

"We all pay our dues, don't we?"

"How did you?"

"Ah! The typical way. Waiting on tables, mostly."

"Really?"

"You never want to be too good at waiting tables because the tips can get pretty good. And then you start to rely on that rather than going out on casting calls. It's hard enough to get rejection after rejection, but when you think about the tips you could be making, it's even harder."

Avalon was about to say something else when two men rushed up to her. It was obviously the director and assistant director because they began to discuss the upcoming shot.

"The stunt director needs you to see him. He has your knee pads," the director said.

"So, I need to change into my other pants."

He nodded at Avalon. "Yes. I think those would show the outline of the pads underneath. Wardrobe is aware of that and they're coming out with the other pair."

Paige still felt nervous and tried to shake the mood off by

grabbing the camera from her satchel and concentrating on the settings. Were her hands shaking slightly because Avalon was so attractive in person? Or was it because she was lesbian? Maybe it was just the heat today.

She laughed to herself. The heat. Yeah, that's what it was.

❖

Paige worked her way around the set, taking pictures of Avalon as she prepared for her upcoming scene. She was careful to avoid interrupting the film crew as they worked and still managed to get some great angles and compositions.

She also shot Avalon's interview with *Entertainment Tonight*, which was an unexpected boon. She could write something about the press angle of marketing films.

The current scene called for Avalon to chase the bad guy down an alley. The director and stunt coordinator walked through the scene with Avalon and Manny, a bit actor dressed like a gang member, in slow motion. They discussed the scene's intent and picked the right movements and the exact spot where she would catch up with Manny and jump on his back to take him down.

The crew placed a thick pad on the ground and would film the takedown from three different angles.

Paige positioned herself behind the camera and a little to the left. For this shot she would have virtually the same view as the camera, and then she'd use any additional takes to get more angles.

After a few full rehearsals, the first assistant director called for the camera and sound to roll, and then the director called for action.

The gang member took off running with Avalon right behind him. As they approached their mark and the pad, Avalon charged Manny and leapt onto his back. Both went down in a tumble and the director yelled, "Cut!"

Paige's camera whirred away, capturing Avalon's tackle in ten frames per second. Manny and Avalon laughed as they helped each other up, and the director went over to give them a few more directions.

Paige was captivated by Avalon's physical agility. She seemed unafraid to fall and genuinely seemed to enjoy the risky feat. Desire stirred in her chest, but she squelched the foolish yearning by clearing her throat. *Keep it on a business level*, she told herself. *Don't go barking up a tree you can't climb*. And then she pictured climbing Avalon. She scolded herself again. Stop already!

The director called for another take, and she was amazed that they let her do her own stunts. With the pad there to catch their fall, it didn't seem too dangerous, but a sprained ankle or broken hand could shut down production. She wondered if a double would handle the more precarious stunts to come. She paused, momentarily disappointed and worried if that would be her only stunt.

The crew filmed the scene four more times before "Cut" was called and the crew began to hustle around, moving equipment and shouting orders to each other.

Avalon approached Paige as she made quick notes on her notepad.

"Did you get anything good?"

"I did, I think," she said as she picked up her camera and showed her some of the shots.

"God, my butt is big," Avalon said.

"No, it's not!" she said a little too quickly.

Avalon's voice became much louder as she said, "It's like you were looking right at my ass."

Embarrassed because people were now turning to stare, she quickly said, "No, I wasn't…really—"

"I assume you know how to digitally remove some of that in post-production?"

"I…I…" Her mouth froze in an open position.

"I was joking." Avalon laughed. "Come on. We're going around the block to shoot the next scene."

Flustered, Paige watched Avalon walk away. Her heart beat quickly and she knew her face had bloomed into a rosy blush. She clamped her mouth shut and hurriedly gathered her things to follow.

❖

Avalon sighed as the heat from the sun warmed her shoulders. It was a gorgeous day, and she had a beautiful photographer following a few steps behind her. Teasing Paige had been almost too easy, and she'd have to remember to try not to do it so much. The photographer seemed very nice, but why wasn't she treating her like every other reporter? Most interviewers she met had more polish and a reserved, almost nonchalant, demeanor, but Avalon knew that underneath, they all wanted the same thing—to scoop a bit of gossip or catch her saying something that would sell more magazines. She was used to that type of behavior, and putting up her guard was second nature to her. But Paige didn't appear to be like that.

And then Avalon realized why she was kidding with her. It was as if she'd been a little schoolgirl with a crush on the new student. Avalon almost chuckled out loud.

Paige sure was enchanting. She had a real sincerity about her, in contrast to the many feigned emotions of genuineness Avalon was used to. She loathed people who tried to act dumb when they weren't, only to praise her when she provided an answer or explanation. And the ones that repeated their questions or tried too hard, hoping to draw out the conversation, made her skin crawl. But Paige was to the point and professional, even when Avalon was joshing her. She didn't say things and then wait to see if Avalon agreed or approved. She seemed simply open, honest, and sincere.

When she rounded the corner of the alley, she stopped and waited.

"Let me carry some of your things," she said when she saw Paige juggling her satchel, camera, and notepad.

"Thanks, but I've got it."

The assistant director jogged over to talk to her, and as the two of them walked away, she realized Paige wasn't following. She turned around. "Come on."

When she'd taken a few steps, she couldn't help but turn around. In a voice loud enough to capture the attention of everyone around them, she said, "You're looking at my ass again."

Paige's mouth dropped open and her mortification tugged at Avalon. Remorse at having embarrassed her stabbed painfully in Avalon's gut. Sometimes, she wanted to duct-tape her own mouth. She reached out. "Let me get that." She took her satchel and the three of them turned west onto Selma Avenue and walked to the next set.

❖

Avalon's little escapade threw Paige off-kilter, certainly not something that should be happening in a business relationship. But Avalon appeared to own the world, and everyone else was just her guest. She seemed so unpredictable—nice at times and then off the wall. She wasn't sure who Avalon really was. She definitely needed to spend enough time around her to write a proficient and in-depth exposition for her book. Was Avalon a stereotypical bad girl? Was she just a little crazy? And, more important, had she just flirted with her?

No, she concluded quickly. That was just Avalon. She now knew that whatever Avalon was going to do would add plenty of color to the writing. However, the notion that she might serve as the butt of some of Avalon's pranks sat thick and tense in her stomach.

They had walked less than a quarter of a block when people

dashed toward them. Two men emerged from a car parked across the street, and another three guys ran up from behind them. Paige instinctively pulled her camera close to her body. They circled around in front of Avalon and she realized that this was a group of paparazzi, swooping down for a vulture's snack. They began to call Avalon's name and ask all sorts of questions. They all were talking at once, the jumble of questions sounding like the excited discord of barking dogs. While the assistant director radioed for security, all she could do was watch.

A lone voice yelled over the rest. "Avalon, are you going back to Club Raunch anytime soon?"

Avalon and the assistant director kept walking, forcing the paparazzi to move backward as they worked.

"They serve great martinis," she said. "What can I say?"

Avalon didn't look up when one of them yelled her name, and it seemed like she wasn't hurrying to get to the set, but something in her voice had changed, as if she'd stiffened a bit.

Cameras clicked as the men jostled for position, and a videographer suddenly pushed forward. "We heard your ex is on vacation in the mountains."

She kept walking but another one said, "Hey, Avalon!" and Paige could see her jaw set with tension.

"Avalon, where do you think Jessica is right now? In a camping tent?"

Avalon's laugh was far from jolly. "Probably facedown in Ricki Lake."

The comment stunned Paige so much she almost stopped. Uneasy about being left behind, however, she hurried along, staying as close to Avalon and the assistant director as she could.

Security quickly approached, surrounding Avalon, the assistant director, and her. They pushed back the cameramen and led the three of them past the sawhorse boundary of the set.

She could hear the paparazzi still calling out, and she

couldn't take a normal breath until they'd reached the safety of some director's chairs, shaded by a huge umbrella.

Avalon was pulled into a conversation with the director and assistant director, leaving Paige to assess the last few minutes.

There it was again, Avalon's unpredictable side. The paparazzi had gone after her to make a buck, all for the sake of selling shots to magazines and television shows. Shoving into her personal space in their relentless pursuit, they prodded Hollywood celebrities about their dirty laundry and dalliances in pursuit of a sellable sound bite.

Facedown in Ricki Lake?

She shook her head. Obviously, they'd just gotten a good one.

❖

The director yelled "cut" and Avalon walked off the set to find Paige. It had been over an hour since she'd seen her, and she hoped she was still on set. As she made her way toward the catering area she heard someone calling her name.

Her manager, Michele D., walked up as briskly as a mailman in the rain. Avalon wasn't surprised at the outfit she wore. The entire Gucci ensemble, replete with gilet jacket, drape-neck top, odalisque pants, and the rather large handbag, had to have cost over $9,000, but she wore it like it was a sweat suit covering her gangly, malnourished frame. Michele was a formidable manager, however, and worth every bit of the 15 percent she took from Avalon's paycheck. Michele used only her initial as her last name, and though Avalon thought it was a bit silly, everyone knew her as Michele D., or "the D." Michele had been her advisor for the last five years and was never too far from a blunt comment or opinion.

"Avalon," she said, stopping less than six inches from her face. Michele was five feet ten, the same height as she was, and those bloodshot eyes were boring directly into hers. "Facedown in Ricki Lake?"

She laughed.

"It's not fucking funny. It'll be on TMZ tonight and there's nothing I can do about it. Harvey Levin won't call me back."

"It's not a big deal, Michele."

"We just got past the Club Raunch fiasco. I don't need this."

"You don't need this? That's what I pay you for."

"You don't need it, either. I thought we agreed a while ago that you'd tone it down. If you keep popping off whenever there's a camera around, you're going to find yourself on the quiet side of a cell phone. Producers and directors don't like bad press from an actress. Jesus! Stop making cracks about Jessica."

If Ricki Lake *were* gay, Jessica would probably have tried something. Jessica couldn't say no, not to any of the women who threw themselves at her or the women Jessica pursued. And many of them came along when they had shared a bed together. Avalon was still hurt and angry, and the memories of Jessica's trysts tightened in an angry knot in her stomach. The tension had eased a little, due to the time and distance between them, but the snide look on that videographer's face when he asked about Jessica infuriated her. He knew goddamn well that Jessica was in the arms of someone else.

She had fallen for his ruse, and now her manager was chewing her ass into a little wad of shame.

"Okay," she said as she raised her hands in surrender. "I'll stop the Jessica comments."

Michele D. switched the Gucci bag to her other hand. "I've gotta try to reach Harvey," she said as she walked away, cell phone already connected to her ear.

Avalon shook her head, relieved that Michele D. was leaving but pissed that she'd been scolded again.

She turned abruptly, snorting her frustration as she headed for the craft service table.

Paige wasn't there, so she checked the catering tent. A number of crew people sat at the tables, but that was all.

When she got to her trailer, she hoped Paige would be there, but the place was as empty as a bank on Sunday.

She got a bottle of water out of her fridge and sat down just as a thumping sound came from the door. A jolt of anticipation at seeing Paige rose quickly through her body but suddenly perished when the second assistant director called through the door.

"You've got about twenty minutes, okay?"

"Yeah," she yelled back.

Maybe Paige had already left the set. An uneasiness settled in her stomach. What if Paige left because she'd kidded her earlier? Even though they'd just met, the possibility that it was because of something she'd said pressed hard against Avalon's chest. The sensation was unfamiliar and it surprised her.

Knuckles rapped on the door again.

"Twenty minutes. I got it," Avalon yelled a little too loudly.

"May I come in?"

It was Paige. "Of course!" Avalon's mood lightened as Paige stepped in. "I'm sorry, I thought you were someone else."

"And you've got twenty minutes, I'm guessing."

The unexpected wisecrack caused her to giggle. "I do, yes."

"I was coming by to tell you I'm done for the day."

"You're lucky. I've got another few hours of what we call 'hurry up and wait.'"

"There's a lot of that on a film set, I've noticed."

"Yeah, and people wonder why a movie ticket costs more than a tankful of gas."

"Thanks for accommodating me today," Paige said.

"Anytime. And hey, I'm sorry if I embarrassed you earlier."

"What? The comment about your ex or the crack about your ass?"

Avalon nodded. "Ass crack, I get it—"

"No!" Paige suddenly said, "I didn't mean it that way!"

"See? I did it again."

Paige laughed and Avalon joined in. She loved how Paige's surprised expression transformed into a squinty-eyed attempt at annoyance, then settled into a sideways smile. She hoped it meant that she hadn't screwed up earlier.

"Just be careful," Paige said, holding up her camera. "This has a macro lens and can proficiently capture nose hairs."

Before she could stop herself, Avalon raised a hand to her nose. She'd been one-upped and she loved it.

"Duly noted, Miss Cornish."

Paige turned to open the door. "See you tomorrow?"

"I hope so."

When the door clicked closed, Avalon sat still, absorbing the silence with the subtle significance of a poet's pause. And like the first swirls of a buffeting wind that precede the rumbling thunder of an oncoming storm, something told her that fate was suddenly not fooling around.

❖

"Wow," Chris said as she looked over Paige's shoulder.

Paige sat in front of the laptop at her desk and clicked through the shots she'd taken earlier on the set. They hadn't been cropped or color corrected, but they were stunning.

Chris flicked open a can of Heineken and sprayed little bits of hops-smelling brew on Paige's neck.

"Thanks," she said as she continued to click through.

"Sorry. These are fantastic, Paige. You could do a whole book on her and I'd buy it."

She nodded. She could fill a few books with these images. Avalon made the pictures almost come alive. Whether Avalon was running, discussing something with the director, or just grinning directly at the camera, she had made Paige forget about who she was photographing, letting her just record the action. Otherwise, she would have stared through the lens in a voyeuristic stupor. "I know. But I still have to arrange meetings with a few other actors to pull this all together."

"So what was she like?" Chris stepped around her to prop her butt against the desk. "Crazy? Ferocious?"

"Amazing. She's gregarious and assertive and untamed." She laughed. "Everything I'm not."

"Maybe a little of that will rub off on you. That is, if you get lucky enough for her to rub anything on you."

She elbowed Chris. "Stop that."

"I'm just sayin'."

"Drop it." She sat back. "But she's really wild, Chris. She spouts off to the press and she doesn't care what she says. I can't explain it exactly, but being around her feels dangerous. I picture the LA River, after a huge rainstorm, and those people who go to watch and fall in. They get swept up by a swift and treacherous current and flail around, but they can't do anything to get out of it."

"I suppose your life isn't your own when you're in the public eye."

"It's a speed I couldn't handle." She pictured Avalon's beautiful face and inviting smile. "She's also very nice. She asked if she could help me carry my stuff."

"Really?"

"I think she did it because she'd just embarrassed me."

"What'd she do?"

"She accused me of looking at her ass."

"Did you?"

"No!"

"I don't believe you. The forces of nature would have pulled your eyes right to her tush."

"Either way, she toyed with me. It felt weird." And she'd also felt exposed, like Avalon knew she'd harbored an impractical and unattainable crush on her.

"She was flirting with you, Einstein."

"She probably does that with everyone."

Chris took a swig from her can as she perused the photos. "I just might have to visit the set. Who knows what crimes are being committed there. I might have to question one Miss Avalon Randolph."

"You see, that's just it. You wouldn't think twice about walking right up to her and starting a conversation. I, on the other hand, am always the one that's ten paces away, just watching."

"But you aren't this time. You're working with her on this book. Just enjoy it and see where it goes."

Frustrated that Chris was only confirming what Paige knew was the truth—a fact that would remain deeply buried, no matter how legitimate—she said, "Why are you assuming it'll go anywhere? You have a bad habit of making romantic connections in just about any situation you see." She lowered the screen of her laptop. "You could matchmake in the frozen-foods section of a grocery store, for God's sake."

"Don't knock it. A whole lot of available people hang out by the single-serving section."

She got up and Chris followed her to the living room. They flopped down on the couch and Chris propped her feet up on the coffee table with a groan.

She nodded toward Chris. "Hurt yourself again?"

"Yeah." Chris grimaced. "A very large and drunk woman decided she wasn't going to listen to my orders last night. She and I had to go to the pavement to discuss the matter further. I wrenched my back when we did our little do-si-do." Chris took another sip. "Jen used to rub my back when I came home. I miss that."

"You miss her?"

"No, not her. I just miss the caretaking. Our relationship never really went anywhere, you know? I never asked her to move in because it just didn't feel right. Except for the back rubs."

"Kind of like me and Marlene."

"Exactly. Apart from the cheating and lying, she was just like Jen."

She scowled at Chris. "I mean the caretaking part. Sometimes Marlene would make dinner or do my laundry…"

"She should have. Hell, she was unemployed the whole three years you were together."

Paige always saw herself as the stable one. She was there to help Marlene. She hadn't really assumed that the gesture would be returned. After all, wasn't that what unselfish love was all about? "She had trouble getting work."

"She had trouble getting out the door to go find work."

"I suppose I made it too comfortable for her."

"No, you were just being a good person. She took advantage of you. You know I've told you before that you don't pay enough attention to your own emotional needs. You're more driven to meet others' needs, and Marlene trampled all over that."

"I was stupid."

"No, she was stupid. Stupid enough to hurt you." Chris nudged her. "Plus, she constantly berated you about every little thing. Don't beat yourself up. Marlene needed to move on and you're better off for it."

"I should have been more encouraging of her career."

"She didn't have a career! She had a whole bunch of pipe dreams. And by the way, you supported her in everything she wanted to do. And she thanked you by dating the women's softball team."

"Excluding the catcher."

Chris laughed. "Only because you caught her before she could finish the entire job. You deserve someone who can't even see the entire softball team because they're too into you."

"Does that exist?"

"I sure hope so." Chris tipped her head back on the couch. "For both of us."

Paige felt the sting of hurt that prickled around her desire for someone just like Chris had described. Someone who would see only her. A few times in her life she'd mistakenly thought that's what she had. And maybe she'd had it for a moment, but it always seemed to leave so cruelly, without once looking back. If there had been enough room on the couch, she might have let herself crumple and curl into a miserable ball.

CHAPTER FIVE

Though the scenes Avalon shot that day were complicated and demanded her complete attention, Paige's presence floated around the edge of her awareness. She wondered what Paige was doing. Was she taking pictures at that moment? Was she making mental notes? Was she thinking about her like Avalon was thinking about her?

"Avalon," the director said as they were readying the cameras to shoot her fistfight with Brent Hastings, her costar, "we'll pick this scene up where the gun has been kicked out of your hand. I'm going to ask Brent to come as close as he can to your face when he throws the first punch. The camera angle is so close to parallel that it will only look good if we do it this way. As soon as he tries to hit you, you bend backward, avoid the blow, and then counter with the kick you rehearsed. You'll have to aim close to his face, as well. Are you all right with that?"

"Sure." These kinds of scenes really excited her. She was new to action movies and wanted to impress the director so she'd be considered for more.

Brent stepped up to her. "You ready?"

"Bring it on, pretty boy." She returned the mega-million-dollar smile before the assistant director told the crew to roll.

"Speed," the sound engineer yelled, indicating that the equipment was ready.

"Action," the director called out.

She looked at the handgun on the ground, reacting to the fact that he'd just disarmed her.

"Evens the score, doesn't it?" Brent's voice was menacing in its condescension.

"Not quite." She sneered as Brent tipped his shoulder back.

Her thoughts jumped and she was wondering whether Paige was getting this on film when a bright light exploded in her head. She fell backward and the back of her head smacked the rough pavement.

She closed her eyes and heard excited shouting, and suddenly someone was bent over her.

"Avalon! Avalon! Are you okay?" She felt Brent's hand on her cheek. "I'm so sorry!"

The director swore at Brent and knelt by her side. "Get the set medic!"

"I'm fine," she tried to say, but a rolling ripple of nausea gurgled in her stomach.

"Stay down," someone else said.

Embarrassed, she stayed where she was, looking up at her repentant costar.

"It was my fault," she told him. "I forgot to move back."

The medic rushed up to her, and while he tended to her, she wholeheartedly hoped that Paige had missed the whole thing.

"You're done for the day," the director said when she was finally allowed to stand.

She had a small cut on her upper cheek that the medic said was already bruising. She had a hell of a headache, but the mortification she felt at her bumble was much more painful. The medic told her to keep the ice pack he'd given her and she reluctantly held it to her face.

"I'm fine, really."

"Back to your trailer. I'll have Penny walk you."

"I'll take her."

Avalon turned to the new voice. Paige stood behind her, camera in hand.

"Shit," Avalon mumbled.

She felt Paige's strong hand encircle her arm. If only the first time they touched could have been more romantic and less embarrassing. She wanted to enjoy Paige's closeness, but the slamming pain in her head kept her from the pleasure.

Damn, she thought, *this sucks in every way but the one where it's Paige that's taking me away from the set.*

❖

They reached the door of her motor home before either of them said anything.

"I don't suppose you were taking a smoke break or otherwise absent during that last scene."

Paige was holding Avalon's elbow, helping her up the stairs and inside. She probably didn't need the assistance, but she accepted it. "I don't smoke."

Avalon tossed the ice pack on an end table and sat down on the couch. "So that means you got it on film?"

"Yup."

She dropped her head in her hand. "Ughhhh."

Paige sat down next to her. "What's the matter? Do you need the medic again?"

"No, my head doesn't hurt. But my self-esteem just got its ass kicked."

"If it's any consolation, it was a fantastic photo op."

Avalon lifted her head and laughed. "Ouch! Okay, my head does hurt."

"What can I do?"

"Delete those pictures."

"Sorry, I can't obliterate true drama."

Avalon squinted in what looked like mock annoyance. "Then

how about going over to that cabinet under the sink and fetching me some medicine?"

"Sure." She jumped up and walked over to the sink. "Am I looking for a bottle of pills?"

"No. You're looking for the bottle of whiskey," Avalon said as she picked up the camera Paige had left on the couch.

"Keep your hands off that," she said without turning around.

"How did you know I had your camera?"

"If it had happened to me, I'd be doing the same thing."

"So you're sympathetic to my embarrassing plight?"

"I am," Paige said as she poured oak-tinged liquid into a small glass. "From awkward moments come graceful pictures."

"Pour yourself some," Avalon said. "Is that some famous quote?"

"I just made it up so you'd leave my camera alone."

Avalon put the camera down and Paige returned with two glasses.

"Here." She handed Avalon one. "I don't know if this will help, though."

"It certainly won't hurt." Avalon raised her glass to her and they both drank.

She grimaced as the liquid singed her throat and smoldered in her stomach. "Wow."

"It's a nice way to end the workday," Avalon said.

After they both took another sip, Paige said, "What's it like to have the paparazzi all up in your grill?"

"A necessary evil, I suppose."

"What did they mean about going back to Club Raunch?"

"You're probably the only one who hasn't heard. That was where my ex and I broke up. It was a bit of a scene. Words and drinks were flying, and a lot of people caught it on camera. The whole scene got pretty ugly."

"I'm sorry you went through that."

Avalon's nod seemed almost philosophical. Paige wondered what was behind that look.

"So, what does a photographer do when she's not looking through a camera lens?"

She had to think for a moment. Her life had been fairly boring lately. "I originally thought I'd get a break after my last book came out. I was planning to take a trip somewhere. I like to go on photo excursions. The best part is getting lost and then finding things that I'd never have photographed if I'd stayed on track. But before I knew it, I was asked to get going on this project."

"You're behind your camera most of the time?"

She laughed, a little self-conscious. "No. I mean I have a life.",

Avalon was watching her, an adorable sideways grin on her face that made Paige's foot bounce in both nervousness and excitement.

"I do!" She couldn't help but grin because she knew the stare was a challenge. "My best friend, Chris, and I do a lot of things together. I bike, sometimes. I..."

Avalon waited, which made it harder for Paige to think of anything interesting.

She looked up, scanning the interior of the motor home for nothing in particular. "Mostly, I've been getting used to being with me again. My lover and I broke up and it was pretty horrible for me." When she looked back at Avalon, a flood of warmth filled her because her expression was so gentle and caring. It also rattled her a bit.

"What happened?" Avalon said.

"I guess the usual breakup. We grew apart. She wasn't the easiest person to live with. Maybe I wasn't, either. She was prone to depression and could get pretty mean. I suppose one too many nasty remarks finally made me see that I was becoming extremely unhappy."

"I'm sorry."

There she was being disarmingly kind again.

"You shouldn't be. I'm glad she's gone. Well, she's not really gone. I mean, she's moved out, but she tried to find me almost every day for a month to tell me how much of a bitch I am."

"For trying to be happy?"

She shrugged. "For not supporting her anymore, I presume."

"Oh, one of those."

"I don't imagine you have problems like that."

"Maybe different problems, but problems just the same. My ex is still around, too. We're in the same industry so it's hard to avoid her at times."

"Jessica Wiley." Who didn't know they had been together? Their relationship had been well covered in the magazines and TV entertainment shows.

"That would be her. Luckily she's been in Toronto shooting a film, so I've gotten a little break. But I guess she's on vacation now."

"Are you two on speaking terms?"

"Not really. She calls me when she wants. I'd rather not be involved anymore because she exhibits a vengeful streak at times, especially when she doesn't get her way." Avalon seemed to grow a bit sad. "It's unfortunate when you can't be friends with someone you loved."

"It must be strange to see her in the news and in magazines."

"I try to ignore a lot of that stuff. I mean, people have to make money and the paparazzi serve a purpose."

"Keeping your name out there," she said.

"Yes. But it's not always a great thing."

"It's got to be hard having your life recorded all the time."

Avalon shrugged. "It's the parsley that comes with your meal. You never want it, but it's always there."

Paige chuckled and made a note to remember that quote for her book.

"I'd ask you what you do when you're not working, but I'm sure the list is a lot longer than mine." She felt a little foolish for asking. It was obvious that Avalon's life was more glamorous than hers, but she didn't have to ask her to spell it out.

"I attend a lot of industry stuff. It's important to network. But I wish I had more time to do some of the things I haven't done for a long time."

"Like what?"

Looking toward the ceiling, Avalon inhaled deeply. "A hike in the mountains, maybe. Or the chance to sit in a bohemian coffee shop and just hang out. And I can't remember the last time I sat around the house in my jammies and no makeup, watching old scary movies on TV."

"Which one, for instance?"

"The Day of the Triffids."

"With Howard Keel," Paige said a little too quickly. She shrugged. "I'm a B-film geek."

"You, too?"

"B films are my weakness, and *The Day of the Triffids* is one of the best."

"Just between you and me, I've never watched a meteor shower since."

Paige laughed. "What else?"

"Hmm. All right, geek, which one is this? Phoenixville, Pennsylvania. Steve McQueen—"

"Too easy. *The Blob.*"

"I love that one! No one believes the teenagers when they're trying to warn everyone about the monster. What a classic."

"Okay, here's one for you," Paige said. "Vincent Price, five unsuspecting people, and a $10,000 reward."

"House on Haunted Hill!"

"I may have met my nerdy match."

"Well, I've been called a lot of things, but I think that's the nicest one I've heard in a long time." Avalon grinned as if she truly meant it. "I like you."

The comment was a little surprising, not because it was out of the blue, but because it appeared that Avalon had just had a revelation. Maybe she didn't run into that many people she truly liked.

Paige emptied the last of her whiskey.

"Want another one?"

"No, thank you."

A knock on the door made Avalon sigh, and Paige liked that she didn't seem to want to be interrupted. Helen poked her head inside the door, telling Avalon that the set medic recommended a trip to her doctor to look at her head.

"I don't think I need it," Avalon said.

"The producers told me they need some paperwork for your injury."

"Tell them they can cover their asses with their own paperwork."

"Seriously?"

"Yes."

Helen paused and then left.

Paige set the glass down on the coffee table. "You don't mince words, do you?"

Avalon shrugged. "My mouth gets me into a lot of trouble sometimes."

"So does your slow reaction to oncoming fists."

Avalon squinted again and looked adorable. "Funny."

"I should go," Paige said as she stood. "Are you going to be all right?"

"My head is fine. And since they're reshooting that scene tomorrow and scheduling other stuff for the rest of the afternoon, I'm done for the day."

She looked at her watch. It was just after two o'clock. "Well, now's the time you've wanted."

Avalon looked at her, apparently not quite understanding.

"Time for you to do what you want to do," she said, then added, "See you tomorrow."

Avalon stood and took a step toward her. "Care to take in a double feature?"

"What?"

"I'll tell my driver to take the rest of the day off. Drive me home and I'll show you."

Was Avalon asking her to go home with her? Was she kidding? Maybe she considered this part of the interview. Maybe the blockbuster actress had hit her head too hard.

Did she want to go home with her? Did jackpots come from slot machines?

"My car's parked on Highland."

❖

Avalon directed Paige east, through the upper-crust neighborhoods of Westwood and Brentwood, down Sunset Boulevard and, finally, to an address on Via De Las Olas Drive in Pacific Palisades. From high in the hills above, the front of the house overlooked Palisades Park and, beyond that, the shimmering, cobalt-blue expanse of the Pacific Ocean.

The house wasn't a mansion by any stretch of the imagination, but rather a typical California-style ranch house built, probably, in the early 1950s, but *typical* ended there. These houses were priced in the millions, given the exclusivity of the neighborhood and the exceptional ocean views.

Avalon took her inside and the comfortable décor impressed her.

"I remodeled the place to resemble what it might have looked like when the house was first built," Avalon said, as if reading her mind.

Blond furniture stood upon a large rug that followed the outline of the room, allowing about six inches of hardwood floor to peek out from underneath. It was a light, pleasant room that captured the spirit of the intended design.

"The interior decorator mixed original fifties furniture with new, retro pieces," Avalon said. "I feel like I'm in a time warp, but a carefree, innocent one, you know?"

It was almost as if Avalon was looking for her approval. "I like it a lot. It's really nicely done."

She liked the exultant feeling Avalon's engaging grin gave her. When Avalon headed toward the open kitchen, she told Paige to seat herself on a low, red couch that looked like it was taken straight from a mid-century modern encyclopedia. The walls of the front room were not light blue or beige, like contemporary houses, but gray. Classic bark-cloth drapes in shades of gray and yellow framed the large windows. It lacked all the unnecessary ornamentation that the 1950s eschewed.

"Form follows function," Paige said as she admired the kidney-shaped coffee table and no-nonsense easy chairs in one corner.

"My designer would love you. She said that in a house like this, there needs to be a seamless marriage between eye-pleasing style and real-world practicality."

The house was probably three or four times the size of Paige's, but not one of those gargantuan mansions that stars were prone to possess. "You've hit the mark, I'd say."

Avalon returned with two glasses of iced tea, served in large tumblers. "Is this okay?"

"Perfect." She took the drink and realized that she was more comfortable than she'd been since meeting Avalon.

Here at home, Avalon seemed relaxed too, and Paige felt the tug of an urge to photograph her that way but resisted the temptation since they'd only just gotten there.

Avalon sat next to her and a rush of exhilaration coursed through her. She was in Avalon Randolph's home, just the two of them. Sure, it was a work assignment and Avalon was just doing the publicity part of her job, but she'd never been to a famous actor's house before, and in her wildest dreams she would never have imagined being invited by Avalon.

"How do you think the movie is coming along so far?"

Paige hadn't really talked to Avalon about that subject, and any comments might be good for the book.

"For my first action film, pretty well, I guess. The crew is really nice and I love the director."

"And Brent?"

"He's great. He teases me a lot, but I think that's his way of telling me he likes working with me."

"Tell me how the action scenes have been."

Avalon sat back and crossed her legs, the glass of iced tea perched in her lap. "We've only done a few, but I love them. Barring the thumping I received today, of course."

"Of course." She wanted to laugh but pressed her lips together to try to staunch the urge. But when Avalon chuckled, she couldn't help but join in.

"I swear," Avalon said, "I'm going to get those images from you if it's the last thing I do."

"That won't be hard."

"It won't?"

"Not at all." Paige paused, then said, "You'll be able to pick up my book at any large chain bookstore and major online retailers."

Avalon squinted and shook her head, but her lovely upturned mouth belied her attempt at a threat.

"Okay, how's this. I'll let you pick the one that goes in my book."

"How many do you have?"

"Oh…" Paige said, mischievously drawing out the answer, "ten."

"Really?"

"No."

Avalon sighed loudly.

"Actually, I think it's more like fifteen or sixteen."

When Avalon groaned, she couldn't help but add, "My camera records at ten frames per second, so be happy that it only took Brent about a second and a half to punch you."

"This is horrible."

"And there are some of you when you hit the ground."

"I'm going to take away your iced tea."

"Plus the ones with you on your back looking up at the sky."

"And send you home."

She laughed. "It will prove to the world that you do your own stunts."

"One of my first action scenes and I end up with a big, honkin' bruise."

She leaned toward Avalon. "It's not that noticeable. But it might be tomorrow."

"Well, I guess that's what makeup is for."

Avalon ordered dinner from some place Paige had never heard, of and as the sun began to set over the ocean, it came, and Avalon spread it out on the coffee table.

Everything made Paige's mouth water.

"I hope you like dim sum," Avalon said as she pointed out each item written in Chinese. "That's bean-curd rolls, shrimp dumplings, and pork spareribs in black bean sauce. Those are vegetarian dumplings, that's vegetable fried rice, and, for dessert, we have papaya in warm rice and coconut juice."

Paige's stomach rumbled as she realized she hadn't eaten since breakfast. Avalon brought a pitcher of iced tea from the kitchen and refilled their glasses.

"I have chosen an insect theme for our double feature tonight," Avalon said as she picked up the remote and pointed it at the largest television screen Paige had ever seen. "The first one takes place in 1954, right after the earliest atomic tests in New Mexico have caused a freakish mutation."

She knew that film and dramatically raised her hand, pointing to nothing in particular as she mimicked the little girl in the opening scenes. "Ahhh! Them! Them!"

Avalon laughed, seemingly pleased, and Paige loved it. She'd watched the film about atomically altered giant ants wreaking havoc on civilization many times and guessed that Avalon had as well.

The film started as she and Avalon shared the dim sum. When the police questioned the little Ellison girl, she suddenly came out of her catatonic state and screamed, Avalon tilted toward her, pushing her shoulder into her. "The delivery of your line was much better."

"Why, thank you." She was floating in her own B-film fantasy, costarring Avalon and Paige. Who knew what adventures they could have.

They both pointed to the screen when the shadow of a sound technician's microphone boom came into view and commented on all of the continuity gaffs, which were plentiful in that type of low-budget movie. It was as if they'd watched this movie together many times. They mimicked lines throughout, and when Jensen got frustrated at the military general, she and Avalon simultaneously bellowed the rest of his lines.

By then, she noticed that Avalon had moved closer to her, and with every laugh, their bodies touched as if completing a magical and exquisite connection between them. She tried not to read much into it, told herself not to make anything of it, but she found it almost impossible.

By the time the police had firebombed the giant mutant ants, the dinner and dessert were long gone.

She stretched as Avalon cued up the next film.

"Can you stay for one more?" she asked, almost childlike. Paige wondered if she was feeling vulnerable for some reason. They'd just laughed through an hour and a half of bad science fiction and now Avalon didn't want her to go just yet.

"I don't think it's healthy to watch only one dreadfully classic movie at a time. And you promised a double feature."

Avalon brightened. "I did, didn't I?"

"What is it?"

Avalon smiled mischievously. "An isolated desert laboratory."

"I need more clues than that."

"1955."

It wasn't enough. "More…"

"An experiment with growth hormones to increase the world's food supply."

"Oh, shoot! It's familiar but I can't place it."

"One more clue. A pretty doctor's assistant whose all-time best line is, 'Science or no science, a girl's got to get her hair done.'"

"Oh, my God! You've got *Tarantula!*"

"In the flesh-eating flesh."

"Score!" This was one film she hadn't seen since she was a teenager, spending a flu-stricken weekend at home with her two younger brothers. But at the time, she had laughed so hard at the "Science or no science" line that she'd coughed herself into a frenzy.

Halfway through the film, Avalon reached for a quilt and wrapped it around them. The night had gotten colder and Paige welcomed the comfort. And when the credits rolled on *Tarantula*, she was surprised that it was after ten o'clock.

She told Avalon that she needed to get home. In truth, nothing was waiting for her there. Her attraction to Avalon had grown, and halfway through the second film, Avalon was no longer the famous actress, but a comfortable and exciting woman who seemed to be responding to her presence. But somehow, it just seemed appropriate that they end the evening there. If she'd read more into the evening than Avalon intended, she didn't want to burst her own bubble just yet. The night had been too perfect.

Avalon walked her to the front door. "I can't remember the last time I had such a great evening. I can truly say that it was better than the Oscars."

They both paused while Paige nervously dangled her keys. Suddenly, the awareness of Avalon's Hollywood status crashed back into her brain. "Tonight wasn't exactly a red-carpet event."

Damn it, she thought. She hated demeaning their time together, but even more, she would hate it if Avalon was just being cordial.

"That's different."

"How?" She'd gone this far, so she might as well find out.

"The food was better," Avalon said. "The films were more entertaining than a lot I sit through, and the company was unrivaled."

Paige didn't know what to say. She wanted to kiss Avalon, just an innocent kiss to say thank you for the night, but at the same time, she was afraid Avalon might lean in for one. She was convinced that if they did kiss, it would mean more to her than to Avalon. After all, Paige had followed Avalon's career and always thought she was incredibly beautiful. And until the other day, Avalon didn't know Paige existed. Maybe Avalon thought she was just a new amusement, someone that could be a fun but fleeting pursuit. Paige didn't want an uncomfortable working environment, knowing the discomfort from some momentary liaison would be hers alone. Actresses of Avalon's caliber had to be used to a certain high standard of lovers: case in point, her ex, Jessica Wiley. Who could compete with that? No, there was too much of a possibility that Paige would end up the short-lived catnip in Avalon's mouse toy. More than that, she didn't care to want something she couldn't have.

"Thank you for everything," she said as a flutter of regret passed through her. She had sounded so diffident.

"We're shooting another car chase after lunch tomorrow. It's the only action scene of the day. See you then?"

She tried to brighten what she knew was a weak and vulnerable smile. "Absolutely."

She walked to the car as frustrated as a six-year-old forced to leave Disneyland. No fluffy toy, no balloon.

And like the child who doesn't want to know that a person lurks inside those costumed characters, she didn't want to know what Avalon might really be like on the inside. Just for tonight, she needed to imagine that Avalon really liked her and had genuinely singled her out.

The pull to stay with her longer still reverberated vigorously in her gut, but she was afraid the bubble might burst and she'd realize that she was just a time-filler for Avalon.

And though the decision to leave came with a flood of regret, she couldn't trust that her longing was reciprocal, so she started the car and pulled out of the driveway, telling herself that leaving was safer than taking a risk and staying.

❖

"Where are you?" Chris was on patrol somewhere in Hollywood, and Paige needed to talk.

"On Curson, off Santa Monica."

"Busy?"

"Just doing paperwork in my car."

"I'm close, can I come by?"

Paige found her easily and parked behind her squad car. Abel barked from the backseat, as he always did when someone approached.

"Stills." Chris gave Abel the order in Dutch and unlocked the passenger door. "What's up?" she said as Paige sat down and blew out a long breath.

"Avalon."

"Is she being a bitchy, self-important superstar?"

"No, just the opposite. I just came from her house."

"Her house? Seriously?"

She nodded.

"So why do you look like someone just keyed your car?"

"She invited me over and we had dinner. We watched some movies and had a great time."

"That sounds horrible."

"But I'm asking myself, what does she want?"

Chris furrowed her brow.

"I know, it sounds stupid. It just seemed…too nice."

"Your ex sure did a number on you."

"No, it's not about Marlene. Avalon's a celebrity. Why is she spending the evening with me?"

"You do know how ridiculous this sounds, don't you?"

She waved her hand, frustrated. "What I mean is, I don't understand how she could be with Jessica Wiley, a damn superstar, and then invite me over."

"Maybe she wants mundane."

"That helps."

"Not you. A mundane time. No crazy parties, no paparazzi. Just a really nice woman."

Paige stared out of the squad car's windshield, listening to the police radio as a dispatcher reported the results of a license-plate inquiry. The voice sounded monotone and routine, kind of like her life.

"Paige." Chris adjusted her gun belt and turned toward her, shifting the computer screen aside to make room for her knee. "Do you like her?"

Star or not, Hollywood or not, she really liked Avalon. Especially when it was just the two of them. "I do."

"Then don't overthink this. Maybe she just wanted to make a new friend. Maybe she likes you more than that. Either way, just chill or you'll make yourself crazy."

She was right. Avalon's star status clouded Paige's judgment and made her hypervigilant. Whatever it was or wasn't, she still had a job to do. And she'd done this before. Hollywood movies and celebrities weren't new to her. This was her third book, and she was becoming a Hollywood regular herself. She couldn't say she was in the industry exactly, but she made her money from the entertainment world and knew her way around a movie set as well as anyone.

She wasn't a groupie and didn't care to make herself

available because of the lure of the luminary. She just needed to remain professional and do her job. If they shared a laugh or two in the meantime, fine. Thank goodness she'd caught herself so quickly. She wouldn't make a fool of herself by thinking she was in Avalon's romantic sights.

CHAPTER SIX

Paige left her house at six thirty in the morning. Skipping breakfast and even coffee, she didn't want to be late for her meeting with Bubba Densman on the set of his cowboy movie. She drove through the high desert to Lancaster, about an hour north of Los Angeles at the edge of the Antelope Valley.

Though the town had begun as a railroad water stop in the 1800s, it now boasted a population of almost half a million people. Still, many outlying areas in the vicinity afforded film crews a dusty desert landscape on which to build a Western set with a backdrop of an uninhabited and seemingly forsaken desert.

She spent the first couple of hours photographing Bubba and an hour with him as they sat in director's chairs and talked about his experience in action films. He was a big clod of a guy with broad shoulders and gargantuan hands. She realized right away that he wasn't as graceful as previous film editors had portrayed him to be. All morning, he'd bumbled about, trying to hit his camera mark and clumsily throwing his weight around as if he were fighting a colossal sack of angry turkeys. But he was gentlemanly, which Paige appreciated.

She got a lot of great pictures of him in a saloon brawl and captured moments when he was discussing a scene with the director as well as sitting alone on a bale of hay, ostensibly contemplating the next scene.

After she thanked him for his time and asked him if she

could return to do more shooting, they parted ways. She began to head for her car but turned around to take one last look at the set. The crew was still busy preparing the next shot. Off set, she saw the back of a hulking figure heading for the craft service table. It had to be Bubba.

Her gut told her to go back, so she got out her camera and caught up with him just as he bent over to examine a table of fairly elaborate hors d'oeuvres. Her timing was flawless as she snapped a number of completely paradoxical photos, focusing on his huge, dusty sausage-like fingers delicately picking up a petite crostini, his pinkie pointing daintily up.

"Perfect," she said with extreme satisfaction, then headed to her car.

❖

Paige found parking on the corner of Hollywood Boulevard and Seward Street, close to where Avalon said they were shooting. Her cell phone rang as she locked her car. "Paige."

"Marlene." She shook her head in annoyance. "What?"

"I need to come get my flat screen. The one in the bedroom."

"That's not your flat screen."

"I wanted the TV, you didn't."

Marlene's sense of entitlement was unbelievable. "I bought the TV, remember?"

"If I hadn't wanted it, you'd never have gotten it," she said as her voice rose quickly. "If you hadn't been so fucking boring in bed, and out, may I say, the TV wouldn't be there at all."

"I'm hanging up now."

"You don't need the TV, Paige."

She pressed the End button and tried to remind herself again to ignore the ranting of a woman who cared only about herself, but it wasn't easy. Her words still hurt.

Tilting her head back, she let the Southern California sun

warm her face. Marlene was obviously pissed and not getting what she wanted. Let her say what she wanted to. Paige took a deep breath, lowered her head, and walked down the street.

Avalon's production company was shooting only one action scene that day, and Avalon had said they'd film it after lunch. Friday traffic had treated her kindly and she was walking up Seward Street at ten minutes past one.

Helen, Avalon's assistant, cleared her with the police officer who guarded access to the set at Seward and Romaine Street.

"She's in her motor home," Helen said. "It's just past the honey wagon. On the right."

The thundering bass from some hip-hop song rumbled so loudly from the motor home that she stopped at the door, not sure what to do. She stared at a sign that read THE LAST STAND—AVALON RANDOLPH. No one could possibly hear her knock because of the noise, so she decided to wait for the song to end. The windows shook like little children who'd just climbed out of a swimming pool. If she waited long enough, maybe the door might just jiggle open on its own.

"That could go on for a while."

She turned to see Brent Hastings standing behind her. His sudden approach hadn't surprised her as much as the knowledge that the biggest actor in Hollywood was a foot from her face. The only other time she'd seen him in person was the day before, but she'd been too busy capturing their last action scene to notice that up close, he had perfect hair and a startlingly chiseled face. But she hadn't remembered much after he clocked Avalon just as startlingly.

"Here," he said, "let me help." He put his hands on the side of motor home and, with all his weight, began to rock the large vehicle back and forth. It picked up some decent momentum and, within a few seconds, the music stopped and Avalon's door flew open and she jumped out, eyes open wide.

When she saw Paige and Brent, she immediately laughed. "I knew that couldn't be an earthquake. Shit, Brent."

"Shit, nothing, Avalon. You were keeping this young lady waiting with that deafening racket you call music."

Avalon turned to look directly at her, smiling widely. "Brent is a sort of old-fashioned kind of guy. He comes from Texas and appreciates his music with more violin and banjo."

"That'd be fiddle and guitar," he said, before stepping toward Paige. "You're the photographer I saw yesterday, aren't you?"

As she nodded, Avalon quickly took her hand and pulled her into the motor home, calling out to Brent. "And no, you're not going to see the pictures from yesterday."

With a click of the door, she was alone with Avalon.

"How's your head?" She followed Avalon to the little kitchen area.

"You tell me." Avalon turned toward her, offering the left side of her face.

"No swelling," she said, "but your bruise looks worse." She winced, not sure if she should be so blunt.

"I thought I was the one who doesn't mince words."

"I'm sorry."

"Don't be. It's refreshing, actually. Want some iced tea?"

"If it's as good as what I had last night, yes."

Avalon beamed widely as she retrieved a pitcher from her refrigerator and poured two glasses. "It should be. I made it myself. I have a lot of talents, Miss Cornish."

"That reminds me of a question I want to ask you."

Avalon handed her a glass and rested her hip against the counter, eyebrows raised expectantly.

"If you couldn't act, what would you do for a living?"

Avalon took a sip and Paige liked the way she seemed to be considering her answer. Her green eyes were bright, the color of the delicate lichen found on river rocks. The lightness of her eyes, framed by the golden blond of her hair, made her appear fair and fragile. Her reputation was far from that, since the tabloids liked to talk about her wicked mouth and her sometimes-fierce manners. But in that moment, Paige felt more than saw that she was relaxed and peaceful.

"I'd be an architect," Avalon said.

"Really?"

She nodded. "Building things, that's what I'd like to do. Being able to create a structure that suits the people who want to live there, or plays to the arc of the sun and feels as if it was grown from the land it's on, would be so satisfying. Homes say so much about a person and their life, or at least they should. Adobes in New Mexico and Craftsman homes in Pasadena make strong statements about how people want to live and what they want to be surrounded by. And I'd like to create places where they feel comfortable and happy."

Avalon looked at her with a gaze so deep, all she could do was take it in and urge her breathing to slow down. In the following silence, Avalon turned to look out the window and appeared to be contemplating something.

"What are you thinking about?"

After a moment, Avalon said, "Finding land and designing my first project. One for me."

"That sounds wonderful."

"What about you? What would you do without a camera in your hands?"

She hadn't expected Avalon to turn the tables. She was supposed to be conducting the interviews. "I don't know. I mean, I guess if I could do anything I wanted..." She wasn't sure if she should reveal any more.

"Come on, what would you be?"

Embarrassing as it was going to sound, she said it. "A live-weather journalist."

"Like a tornado chaser?"

"Tornadoes, hurricanes, monsoons, yeah."

"Truly?"

"Well, I know I'll never do that, but it would be awesome."

"But why wouldn't you do that?"

She had to laugh at herself. "Because it's not me. My life is fairly predictable and pretty habitual, which is the opposite of what it would have to be if I reported on the world's insane climate."

"That would be so cool to do that!"

She was struck by Avalon's passionate interest in her dream. "Yeah," she said, "but I never will. It's a fantasy that I have for the simple reason that it would force me to be a little more impulsive."

"Feh." Avalon waved her hand in the air as if shooing a fly. "Impulsive is easy."

"For you, maybe. It doesn't come easily to me."

"You just have to not think too much about what you're about to do."

"You mean, like the consequences?"

Avalon pursed her lips and Paige knew she was being scolded for being so stiff, which she was.

"Like the regret that hits you when you realize you could have done something exciting or spontaneous, and didn't."

"Yeah," she said, shaking her head. "I'll leave that to the fearless people."

"You don't think you're—"

Someone knocked on Avalon's door.

"Come in," she called.

Tawnya poked her head in. "Gotta get you ready. Your call is in fifteen." She walked in holding a satchel and dropped it on the counter. As if this routine was as familiar and automatic as walking over to the coffee condiment stand, Avalon relocated to the director's chair in front of Tawnya.

"Now let's see how we're going to cover that cut and bruise of yours…"

When Paige stood and walked toward the door, Avalon said, "You don't have to leave."

"I need to download some images to the laptop in my car." That wasn't really true. She could do that anytime. She was just feeling a little foolish for revealing her crazy dream and needed to get away. "I'll be back before you start shooting."

Avalon watched the door close from its reflection in the mirror she was facing, ignoring the smirk on Tawnya's face behind her.

"You don't have to leave…?" Tawnya brushed out the ends of Avalon's hair.

"She's cute, huh?"

"Very much so."

She fidgeted when Tawnya didn't say any more. Something about Paige was refreshing, and she was miles above her ex in class and decorum. Jessica Wiley was a wild ride, all right, generating more press-covered stories than even she had. There had been instant sparks between them but no lasting fire. She knew that thought seemed silly, but it was like their relationship just materialized overnight. She was pushed onto a roller coaster that she hadn't even asked to board.

Her nerves were always a bit on edge with Jessica, which surprised Avalon because she knew she had her own untamed and spontaneous streak. However, the pairing had seemed so contrived and taken for granted by not only Jessica, but her friends, the press, and just about everyone else.

Paige was a breath of crisp, clean mountain air in a town more noted for its belching car exhaust of a dating pool. The photographer had no pretenses and seemed so…normal.

Sure, Paige had been timid when they first met, a bit nervous even. That reaction wasn't new to Avalon, who'd seen her share of faint-hearted fans and even more jumpy, excitable ones. But Paige seemed to be cut from a different cloth. There was something about her that, though she couldn't quite pinpoint it, was definitely intriguing and worth discovering.

"And?" Tawnya interrupted her musings.

"What?"

"And…what about her, beyond her being cute?"

"I'm just saying that she's cute, that's all."

"I know what that means."

Avalon started to turn around to face her but Tawnya pulled her hair, forcing her back around with a wince. "Ouch. So what's it supposed to mean?"

"Jessica will soon be but a distant, yet pissed-off, memory."

"She's already a memory. Who cares if Jessica's got a stick up her ass? She has no right to my business anymore."

Tawnya brushed the last few tendrils of hair and lightly sprayed them. "If I know anything about her, you'll care."

"Well, I don't."

"I'm not saying you should. She didn't treat you well. I'm just telling you to be careful. She doesn't take rejection too well."

Avalon stood and assessed her image in the mirror. "In this town, who does?"

❖

The one action scene they were filming that day involved a reshoot of yesterday's fistfight. Paige positioned herself close to the same spot she'd been yesterday when Brent Hastings had hit Avalon.

"Ready for more?" Brent said to Paige.

"Yes, as long as more doesn't mean actual contact."

Brent grimaced. "I still feel so bad about that. She's a trouper, but it had to have been painful."

Avalon arrived as the director stepped from behind the camera.

"Same positions," he said, and turned to Avalon. "Are you feeling up to doing this again?"

She raised her arm, wrapping it around Brent's neck. As she pulled him down and locked him in a playful chokehold, she said,

"Absolutely, but let's try to get this right. I don't want to injure my costar's knuckles again."

Laughter erupted from the crew, and the director moved back to stand next to the director of photography.

Paige lifted her camera to frame the shot and saw that Avalon was looking right at her. The smoldering smile weakened her knees so much she almost forgot what she was there to do.

The director called for action, and Avalon and Brent began their scene.

Paige's camera clicked frames in rapid succession. She might be able to string together a series of shots of Avalon ducking from the incoming blow and then countering with an evil roundabout kick. It would be great to include in the book.

The director yelled "cut" and Paige lowered her camera. She was excited about the batch of pictures she'd just taken, but her heart raced about something else. Avalon looked her way again and winked. Her heart rate shifted into double time, leaving no doubt about what that something else was.

❖

The wink came so naturally that Avalon was only aware after she did it. Paige grinned and Avalon liked the connection. But simple reactions like that, she thought as she made her way to her director's chair off set, were the only responses she had gotten from her the night before. It wasn't that she wanted to literally jump on Paige, really. She was just used to something happening. Some romance would have been great, but she had to admit she'd had a fantastic time simply hanging out and watching the movies.

She sat down and waved off Helen's offer of a bottle of water.

Paige struck a melodic chord in her. If instant attraction existed, Avalon had experienced it, and she jerked a little as a thrill scampered up her spine.

She didn't know much about Paige's personal life. She'd talked about a breakup, but Avalon assumed that someone as amazing as Paige had to be dating again.

What would whoever she was dating be like? Would she be just like Paige—reserved, serious, and beautiful? Like she was using a pencil on paper, the picture of a gorgeous woman reclining on a sumptuous love seat sketched itself in her mind. Frowning, she imagined thick eraser lines blotting it out, and a new drawing emerged of an ugly, hunchbacked female gnashing her hideous teeth.

That was better.

"Avalon?"

She looked up to see the assistant director.

"They're ready for your next scene."

Maybe she wasn't dating anyone in particular. On the lucky chance she wasn't, would Paige accept a formal date?

As she made her way to the set, Tawnya fiddling with her hair as she walked, a sudden but strange wave of doubt overcame her. This was a new and strange feeling for her. It sat as uncomfortably as an unripe banana grumbling in the bottom of her stomach.

Maybe she wouldn't.

CHAPTER SEVEN

Come on," Paige heard Avalon say when she'd come back from some discussions with the director.

It was the last shot of the day. Beyond the klieg lights that brightly illuminated the small area of street where the movie cars sat, the sun that had disappeared over the buildings on Hollywood Boulevard now cast an eerie darkness. The surreal daylight of the set made for ideal photographs in a business where Hollywood often altered time and space.

"Where?"

"Just come."

Avalon led her to an Audi TTS. Crew members scurried about, adjusting lights and reflectors, measuring distances from the camera, and calling out orders and remarks.

"Mack, this is Paige. Paige, Mack, our best stunt man."

She shook his hand, though she didn't know why.

Mack reached into the backseat of the car and pulled out a helmet. "Here."

She took it. "What's this?"

"A brain bucket," he said.

"But why am I holding it?"

"I'm not sure, since it should be on your head."

Avalon took it from her. "You're going to be on a ride with us." She began to put the helmet on Paige's head.

"What?"

"You wanted good shots, so you're gonna get some from close up."

"In this?" The car looked dangerous. As she allowed Avalon to help her into the helmet, she nervously sized up the car as if it had just challenged her to an after-school fight. Its polished red paint job covered what Paige thought must be a monster engine. "This looks fast."

Mack nodded, almost indifferent. "265 horsepower, 258 pounds per foot of torque, an inline four-cylinder, spark-ignition engine, double overhead camshafts, and an S model turbocharger. It's a canyon carver."

"We're driving through a canyon?" She knew she sounded ridiculous, but she was having trouble processing this.

"No, silly," Avalon said. "He just means it rips."

"I can get some great shots from the curb."

Avalon pulled her aside, almost intimate in her manner. "Consider this a form of tornado chasing. Don't think about it. Just go with it."

She bit her lip to trap words that would beg them to let her back out. Mack positioned her in the backseat and belted her in. Avalon climbed into the driver's seat, and Paige was glad she couldn't see how scared she was.

While the camera crew adjusted the rigging of one camera on each side of the front windows—one to shoot directly at Avalon in the driver's seat and one to shoot her forward point of view and the car she was to chase—she tried to ready her own camera through hands that shook so badly, she dropped her lens cap. Mack climbed in the backseat and sat beside her.

He must have read her look of horror as one of confusion because he said, "We're not in the shot. And I'm here to help if Avalon gets into trouble."

Her fight-or-flight response had already chosen the latter. "What kind of trouble?"

He shrugged. "If she swerves out of control or hits her head and gets knocked out."

She knew her face hadn't changed, but Mack must have finally noticed the meaning behind her true expression.

"Don't worry. This car has roll bars built in. If we go over, just hang on and go for the ride."

Was he serious? She still had time to back out. But before she could grab the door handle, Avalon turned around and said, "This'll be a blast!"

She knew immediately that the smile she attempted looked more like she'd passed gas because Avalon laughed.

"You'll be fine! I swear!"

"I'm not sure my pants will be." She looked around for something to hang on to but realized she'd need both her hands for shooting. Marlene's cruel words came back to her. *If you hadn't been so fucking boring in bed, and out…*

Well, fuck her. She clenched her jaw and decided to prove her ex wrong.

The director came over to talk to Avalon, and sooner than Paige wanted, she saw the director back away, yell for the cameras to roll, and Avalon hit the gas.

The car sped up rapidly and she was pushed against the backseat. Avalon followed the car in front of her, turn for turn, and Paige thought she was getting a bit too close.

She got some shots off, glad to have adjusted the shutter speed because she was bouncing around pretty well. She was just starting to feel a little more relaxed when the car in front slammed its brakes and Avalon followed suit. Her car spun three hundred and sixty degrees, the tires screeching in what sounded like angry pain. Page closed her eyes, waiting for impact.

The car came to a stop and the first thing she heard was the radio sitting in the front seat cackle. "Cut! That was great!"

"Whooo-hooo!" Avalon yelled. "Fucking awesome!"

"Zero to sixty in three point six seconds," Mack said, as if he were sitting on a couch having coffee with friends instead of in a car that had just spun around faster than Michelle Kwan on Olympic ice.

"Mother of God," Paige murmured as Avalon drove back to their starting point.

"You okay?" Avalon asked when she'd shut the engine off.

The director and some other crew members were walking over to the car while Paige was trying to discern whether her pants were still dry.

"Yeah."

"Get any good shots?"

"I'm not sure."

"Let's get another take of that for good measure," the director told Avalon.

"That's my cue." Paige got out of the car, turning to thank Mack for his help.

"How was the tornado?"

She turned to see Avalon's white teeth gleaming. She was certainly in her element, one so foreign to Paige and one she had just experienced, though she still wasn't sure what she thought of it.

"I can say that was a first."

"Wanna go again?"

"No, no, I got more than I bargained for! Plus, I'm meeting Tawnya in her trailer for an interview."

Avalon's smirk was endearing. "Don't believe everything she tells you."

Paige steadied her still-shaking legs as she walked away. "I will."

The short detour to the craft service table to grab a bottle of water provided a moment for reflection. Never before would she have even considered taking a ride like that. That kind of escapade was for crazy, spontaneous people. But she'd allowed Avalon to coax her into the experience like it was a kiddie's carousel ride.

And she'd survived it! Admittedly, her heart had threatened to hurdle out of her mouth, followed closely by her last meal, but once they were screaming down the street, she felt like a true daredevil.

The exhilaration left her gleefully full, like a tire inflated to the brim and bulging with fresh air.

❖

Tawnya's hair-and-makeup trailer was a double-wide room with makeup chairs and mirrors on one side and couches on the other. The tables under the mirrors were packed with hair spray, brushes, combs, eyeliner, blush, and tissue boxes. Pictures of Avalon, Brent, and the other actors were taped to the walls as reference so Tawnya and her team could keep track of the actors' appearance continuity between scenes.

Paige stepped in and Tawnya greeted her with a hug. She wore skinny black jeans and a red-and-white top that hugged her tall, thin frame. "Hello, Miss Photographer."

"It's Paige."

"Oh, I know that. It's nice to see you again. Would you like something to drink?"

"No, thank you."

"Well, let's sit down, then. My dogs are killing me." She moved two cardboard boxes off the couch to make room and placed them on top of a large pile of similar boxes stacked high against the wall.

"Thanks for taking time to talk to me."

"My pleasure," Tawyna said.

"So, what is your primary role?"

"I'm Avalon's hair stylist and makeup person. Brent Hastings has his own stylist and makeup artist as well. The rest of the actors use a team of others. We work closely with the director, costume designer, and director of photography on the overall look of the character based on the script and the individual scenes. Since we shoot the scenes out of order, we need to maintain continuity. We might shoot the beginning of a scene on one day and finish the scene a week later, so we need to match the actor's look."

"What's it like working with Avalon?"

"She's like a sister to me. We gab and gossip about a million different things."

"Do you ever change a look from what's originally intended?"

"The director and I talk a lot about that before we start shooting. He has the vision for the character and I give him choices. If Avalon has ideas about certain aspects, they'll both talk to me."

"What's the most challenging aspect of your work?"

"I've been doing this a long time, so it's all pretty easy now, but I guess the long hours. The weather can also be a pain. Humid days wreak havoc on makeup and hair."

She looked around the room and paused when she saw the twelve or so boxes. "You must go through a lot of supplies."

Tawyna chuckled. "Those aren't supplies. That's canned food, sweaters, toothbrushes and toothpaste, shoes."

"For the crew?"

"No, they're Avalon's. She didn't have room in her motor home." Tawyna must have noticed that she looked confused because she elaborated. "Avalon delivers all of this to the homeless."

"By herself?"

"Yeah. She loves LA and is pretty fearless about some of the more dangerous neighborhoods. Every month or so, she loads up her car and drives around Skid Row, the LA Mission, places like that, and gives out all that stuff. She knows that a lot of the homeless people have mental illnesses, and she's careful, but she believes that what she does creates kindness in return. Many people know her car now and understand she's not there to hassle them but to help."

"I didn't know that."

"Not many do. And please don't write that down. It's not something she wants advertised."

"Why?"

"Charity isn't about what you get in return. And she doesn't care about those who say charity keeps people from doing for themselves. She says some people are just trying to survive to get to the next day."

Paige stared at the boxes. A flurry of attraction swirled around inside her at the realization that this untamed woman, who was quick with a snarky comment or a brazen observation, had an extraordinarily generous and benevolent side. Avalon worked the publicity machine vigorously, and it seemed that her whole life spilled out onto its pages daily, but the media didn't know it all. Having the privilege of knowing such an important secret made her feel almost reverent. She took in a deep breath to absorb the extremely appealing grasp of Avalon's undisclosed benevolence.

There seemed to be a lot more to Avalon than the rowdiness, and Paige was positively intrigued.

❖

When the crew broke for the evening, Avalon found Paige under the catering tent drinking a Coca-Cola.

"How are you doing?" she said as she sat down at the portable table, next to her.

"Good."

Avalon gestured to Paige's soda. "Mind if I have a sip?"

"Of course not."

With guilty pleasure, she tipped the can and felt wickedly criminal as the sugary liquid quenched her thirst. She handed Paige the can. "That was amazing."

Paige's eyebrows rose and looked like little levitating magic carpets hovering over her eyes.

"Non-diet drinks are an immoral sin in this industry." She shrugged.

"I got some great images of you from the car chase."

As Paige flipped through the pictures on her camera, Avalon bent close. Fresh lavender and spicy vanilla filled her nostrils. It must have been from Paige's shampoo and she moved even closer. Paige noticed but didn't seem to mind, so she balanced herself with an arm around the back of Paige's chair.

"I like that one," she said, pointing to an image of her behind the wheel. It was from Paige's vantage point and clearly captured the car she was chasing in a perfect speed-filled blur.

"I like that one, too. But here are some others…"

"You're really good," Avalon said after they'd gone through most of the day's shoot.

Paige continued to advance the frames. "Thank you."

Leaning back, she said. "Ever think of doing a book or something?"

"That's a really good idea!"

"I thought so. That's why they call me the smart one."

Paige laughed and Avalon felt better. She'd been worried since Paige had gotten out of the Audi. Though the way Paige escaped from the car and almost staggered away had been absolutely adorable, it had also concerned her. She feared that her decision to invite her along hadn't gone well and had actually turned Paige off to spontaneity and adventures.

"Was it worth the shots? The ones from inside the car, I mean?"

"Yes, very much so," Paige said. "In a million years, I wouldn't have asked to go along with you. But now I not only have some good ones to choose from, I have a memento of my daring deed."

"You do! And I'm proud of you for going."

"Did I pass the test?"

Avalon couldn't help but throw her arm around Paige's shoulders and pull her in for a hug. "With flying colors!"

"I'm just glad," Paige said, "that no flying colors came out of my mouth when you spun the car."

She laughed and Paige joined in. That simple expression filled her with a giddy kind of joy. She really liked this woman, and the feeling was as fresh and light as an ocean buoy on the most peaceful of days.

"I need to get going," Paige said as she got up.

"Thanks for being a good sport earlier."

"Thank you for pushing me."

"When will I see you again?"

"I got a copy of the call sheet. You're not shooting any action scenes."

Avalon hadn't even thought to check her schedule for Monday. "Bummer."

"Personally, I'm glad to get a rest from your stunt work."

Paige's smirk made her chuckle. "Are there going to be any more interviews?" She didn't want to sound too hopeful, but she was.

"Yes. I need to get some time with you. Maybe I can come by the set Monday?"

"That'd be great."

Paige walked over to her satchel, which sat on a chair at the end of the table.

The desire to invite Paige over to her house again was strong, but she didn't want to appear too pushy. She believed that Paige had had a good time watching the horror films; however, today she had seemed a little more reserved. Maybe she did have a new girlfriend. Avalon definitely wanted to find out.

Every woman she'd ever taken a liking to made quick work of her intentions. She couldn't remember ever making the first move. If she admitted that out loud it would sound conceited, but actually she felt that her string of exes formed a sort of mundane pattern. In hindsight, it appeared that they enjoyed the excitement of the pursuit because she always seemed to be the one being chased. And sometimes she just went along with the pairing because the women had put out such effort, often to the extreme. It wasn't that she didn't like it, because it always made her feel desired, but it certainly felt rather one-sided.

It seemed so silly, looking back on those times, but a simple fact remained. She wasn't a pursuer.

Paige was about twenty feet away, bending over her satchel. The lower angle from Avalon's chair afforded her a greater appreciation of Paige's backside. Her jeans were tight and she watched some pretty captivating muscles flex as she stood back up. Paige turned to wave and walked away.

Maybe deep down, she thought as she continued to watch Paige, she could be a pursuer.

"Who was that cute thing following you around today?"

Avalon looked up to see Michele D. "How long have you been here?"

"I stopped by a while ago to see how you were doing."

"And you're just now coming over to say hi?"

"You were kind of busy."

"Since when did that ever stop you?"

"So who is she?"

"A photographer. Paige Cornish."

"Magazine?"

"Book."

"A book? That's pretty haughty."

"Since when are books haughty?"

"Since that time you said they were."

"I've changed my mind."

"As you're inclined to do. Listen, I also came by to tell you that you have an interview with the *Hollywood Insider* TV show. They're coming to the set Monday and I'll get them to you."

"Okay."

Michele D. stared at her. Avalon knew that although she'd changed the topic, her manager was thinking only about who the hell Paige Cornish was and what trouble she would cause. Twisted claws of accusation poked Avalon's gut. Michele D. had to have been born from a venue of turkey vultures. Her excellent sense of smell was highly adapted, and it continually annoyed Avalon that she felt like the fresh road kill that wafted into Michele D.'s olfactory bulbs.

Michele D. squinted her beady eyes.

"What?"

"Nothing. I'll see you next week."

Chapter Eight

Carmen Garza's publishing office was in a Spanish-revival building at the corner of Sunset Boulevard and Larrabee Street in West Hollywood. Made up of over 40 percent gay men, the population of West Hollywood also included movie and TV stars, musicians, and bohemian types, all of which Carmen had told Paige were some of the creatively inspiring reasons she had selected that business address. Steps away from the legendary Whiskey a Go Go and just down the street from the Virgin Megastore, also the former and legendary Schwab's Pharmacy, her office overlooked the famous Sunset Strip, sharing the sidewalk with boutiques, restaurants, and nightclubs, all catering to those on the cutting edge of the entertainment industry.

Paige arrived for her Friday-afternoon appointment and was led into Carmen's office. An extension of the architectural style of the exterior, Carmen's work space had a warm and traditional look that reflected her personality. The red-and-gold brocade fabric on her couch and side chairs offset the white stucco walls with hand-painted tile baseboards, the dark wood ceiling beams, and wrought-iron chandelier and sconces. Lush cinnamon-brown drapes framed her arched windows.

"How are you, darling?" Carmen said when Paige sat down. She called everyone darling and treated everyone with the same sentiment. Carmen Garza, a sturdy, middle-aged woman with salt-

and-pepper hair and big bosoms, had a commanding presence. Her pair of designer glasses hung from a chain around her neck like a whistle on a policeman.

"Great."

"*Cut to the Chase*, how's it coming?"

"It's coming."

"I know I'm pushing you on the deadline. It's a short time to get this one to the printer, but you know I have good reasons for that."

"Three months is a challenge, but I've got something to propose."

Carmen raised a pen to her mouth, waiting.

"There aren't many action movies shooting now, but Avalon Randolph is starring in one."

"Avalon? The movie star?"

"Yes. I'm guessing this will be a big publicity move, too. Not a lot of people are talking about it yet. The producers are keeping a lid on it deliberately."

"She's certainly built for the big screen. She's beautiful."

More than you can imagine, Paige thought. "I'd like to focus the majority of the book on her."

"Are there a lot of action scenes?"

She nodded. "And she's doing her own stunts."

Carmen dropped the pen from her lips. "She is?"

"Insane, huh? I can count the number of actresses that do that. And for her first time out, I think I could get a great story. I happened to be there to photograph Brent Hastings accidentally punching her in the face. She's okay, of course."

Carmen nodded her head in silence, obviously deep in thought. "Who else are you shooting?'

"Only Bubba Densman and Ricky Boswell." That's all she had to work with, given the fact that Carmen would be punching the time clock in less than three months.

Carmen nodded again, tapping her pen on the desk. "So,

a more female-centric book on a male-dominated subject," she finally said. "I like it."

Paige was relieved. She didn't have a lot of other options at this point.

"I assume you'll be delving further into Avalon's life? Documenting her home, her free time?"

"Sure." For some reason, the knowledge that she'd already been to Avalon's home felt like a secret. It seemed silly, but Carmen would have asked her what kind of pictures she'd gotten and, frankly, she hadn't gotten any.

"I think a spread with her at one of Hollywood's icons would be good, too."

"You mean, like, the Magic Castle or the Hollywood Bowl?"

"Possibly. There's also Grauman's Chinese Theatre."

"I'd like to go somewhere a little more off the tourist path." She thought a moment and said, "Chateau Marmont."

"Perfect. The stories of Belushi in his garden bungalow and Howard Hughes spying on beautiful women from the attic are legendary, but most people have never been there."

"Most people can't afford the room rates."

"All the more reason it remains exclusive. I'll call ahead and clear the way for you to get a bungalow. And some poolside shots would be marvelous."

The idea was a good one. And illustrating a broader picture of Hollywood moviemaking would allow her to expand upon the theme.

"Thank you, Carmen."

"Three months." She checked her watch. "Minus one week."

"I'll get it done."

"You're my star, Paige."

"Avalon's the star. I just take the pictures and write the text."

"But you're about to be a star in your own right," she said, putting her glasses on. The chain jangled like change in someone's pocket.

"What do you mean?"

"After we go to press, I'm scheduling you for a book tour, darling. We'll expedite the printing of *Cut to the Chase* and get ready for a super-busy schedule of book readings and signings with all three books."

"No!" Paige almost yelled her response, but it came out more like a screech.

Carmen's eyebrows rose and she looked out from the top of her glasses. "No?"

"I mean, no shit!"

"Okaaaay." Carmen looked down at some paperwork. "I'll have the publicity department call you. Plan on going as soon as your book hits the shelves."

Paige managed to get out of Carmen's office before the bonfire of fear raging inside her heated up to a complete meltdown. She tried to take deep breaths, even opening her mouth to gulp in some emergency relief, but nothing helped.

She got outside and looked out onto Sunset Boulevard. Shiny, expensive cars passed with purpose as a faint, cool wind blew in from the direction of the ocean.

Clutching her car keys, she contemplated a hasty disappearance act by driving out of town and not stopping until she reached some place where she could hole up with a bottle of booze and a dead cell phone. But those flights of fancy were reserved for people a lot less rational than she.

Still, her breathing came with effort as she tried to remember where she'd parked.

She closed her eyes and said to no one, "I'm in deep doo-doo."

Chapter Nine

Avalon gazed out over the expanse of the Pacific Ocean. The sea was calm that day and the marine layer was burning off quickly. Soon the sun would warm the water. How wonderful it would feel to be in a beach chair with her toes dug in the sand.

"And as soon as I can arrange it, you'll meet with Garrett Chain. He's directing a huge production in Spain. I told him you'd be interested." Billy Woods paced the floor. He did that quite a lot.

Helen had been in the middle of reviewing Avalon's schedule when Billy came by. Helen now busied herself with something on her iPad while Avalon listened to Billy with partial attention. His job was to take care of things, and details were considered things.

Turning from the window, she crossed the path that Billy paced and sat on the couch. She tapped a rapid staccato on her thigh as she stared at her cell phone on the coffee table. With her toe, she moved it aside from what it had been sitting on—Paige's business card.

"Avalon?"

"Hmmm?"

"This is big."

"I know it is."

"I mean really big."

Her eyes stayed transfixed on the card. "Of course."

"You could easily double your salary. That is, if *The Last Stand* does well. Which it will."

"Uh-huh." What was Paige doing at this very moment? Was she off photographing others for her book? If she had a new girlfriend, was she making her brunch?

"So it's a go, then?"

She looked up. "Sure."

"I'm also asking that you get approval of the male lead."

"Righty-o."

"Great. I'll be off, then."

As Billy let himself out the front door, she picked up Paige's card. She fingered the raised ink, thinking about Paige's skin and how soft it might be. Snippets of her wide and brilliant smile over the last few days cascaded through her mind, one after the other, like a parade of brightly colored floats on the Fourth of July.

❖

Paige sat nervously waiting for Chris to join her at Cecil's, their favorite beer joint. It was crowded for a Saturday afternoon, but she'd grabbed two seats at the bar. She usually stayed with Diet Coke, but a strong, stout ale sat in front of her, half-gone.

"I got your cryptic but anxious text," Chris said as she sidled onto the bar stool next to her. "What's the hubbub about?"

"My publisher is scheduling me for a book tour."

"Public speaking?"

She nodded, too afraid to say it out loud.

Chris caught the eye of the bartender and crooked her thumb toward Paige. "I'll take whatever she's having." She turned back to Paige, shaking her head. "That's like Harrison Ford hanging out with rats."

"Exactly." She took a deep breath. "I can't do…*that*."

"You're an author. You have to sell your books."

"Isn't that what the Internet is about?"

"Selling means reading in front of people."

This time she whispered, as if the boogeyman were right behind her and she had to run. "I can't do that."

The air suddenly grew thin and she sat up straighter. A low buzz filled her ears. She'd been in college the last time she felt this way, but it was happening again. She gulped and opened her mouth, like a pitiable fish thrown from a tank.

"Are you okay?" Chris was looking at her.

She waved her hand in front of her. "Panic...attack."

Joining the debate team her senior year had been a bad idea. During her first debate, she had looked out toward the faces staring back and was sure they were filled with malevolent expectancy. They were there to judge her. She had frozen. The entire classroom went still and the strange ragged noise of wood being cut with a serrated knife filled her ears. She realized it was her own labored breathing and she was losing air fast. Panic overtook her, and the next thing she knew, she was running from the podium, trying to find the first receptacle she could vomit in.

That day, only a handful of people was there. A book tour would have lots more people in much bigger rooms.

Oh, fuck.

"Breathe," Chris was saying.

Look at the bar top, she told herself. *You're in a bar with Chris.*

Way too slowly, her breathing returned to normal and the ear-ringing stopped, but she was damp with sweat. The bartender delivered Chris's beer, and Paige lifted hers and practically drained it as she held up one finger to order another.

"Easy there, Turbo. It's only four p.m. Listen. Maybe you could go to a shrink or get hypnotized. There are ways to get over stage fright."

There was no way she could ever get up in front of people. That's partly why she was a writer and photographer. She could send out her words instead of speak them and could remain on the non-flash end of a camera. "I don't see that anything would work."

"Well, you've gotta try."

Her second beer was brought over and she cradled it as if clinging to a lifesaver on the *Titanic*.

"How am I gonna do this? It's less than five months away. I'm supposed to go out on the road, for gosh sakes. Talk in front of *people*." A sudden chill streaked from her spine to the top layer of her skin, and she shook as badly as if a tooth filling had hit foil.

"Xanax?"

"Well, I guess that's a possibility. I would be facedown at the bookstores and just sleep through the entire tour."

"Yeah, I forgot you're a lightweight."

She swallowed another big gulp of liquid courage, hoping if a little buzz washed over her, the situation might not seem so desperate.

"Keep going like that and you'll be the next Ernestine Hemingway."

"Okay, you're not helping."

Chris swiveled her stool and faced her. "This is something you have to do to help yourself. There's a way, you just have to find it."

"I seriously don't think I—" Her cell phone rattled underneath her car keys. She lifted it off the bar top and saw that the phone number was unfamiliar. "Hello?"

"Paige?"

"Avalon?"

Paige ignored Chris's reaction, which was a perfect imitation of a choirboy's face as he tried to hit a high note.

"Am I interrupting you?"

"Not at all," she said. She didn't want to miss a word, so she plugged a finger in her other ear to minimize the bar noise. Chris elbowed her, mouthing, "That's Avalon? What does she want?!"

"Would you like to go out with me? On a date?"

Stunned, she dropped her finger from her ear and knew her mouth had dropped open.

Now Chris was saying, "What's happening?" so Paige swung around, slapped her knee, and made her most furious face.

"Paige?"

"Yes? I mean, yes, I'd love to."

"Are you free tonight? I know it's rude to give such short notice, but—"

"Tonight's fine."

"May I pick you up?"

She gave her the address, running frantically through the apartment in her mind, making a huge list of what she had to clean and straighten. It had been a hellhole recently and Chris had been her only recent visitor.

"How about seven tonight?"

"That'd be great."

She hung up and stared at the phone. If she had had any more to drink, she would have thought the stupor had her imagining that Avalon Randolph had just phoned.

But she really had.

"What?" Chris was bouncing on her stool. "I take it that was Avalon Randolph, but why was she calling you?"

"We're going on a date tonight." She tried on those words and they felt too surreal. The words *Avalon Randolph* and *date* together in the same sentence sounded as unrelated as salami and raisins.

Chris's choirboy look was there again. "Get the frick outta here. Seriously?" She started looking around the room.

Paige quickly slapped Chris on the arm. "You're not telling a soul."

"Day-yum! This is unbelievable! I'm freaking out here."

"You're freaking out? What about me?" At that moment, speaking in public seemed a long ways away. She knew that particular anxiety had ample time to fester and grow to a full and respectable panic outbreak, but for now, she had a house and body to scour. Avalon Randolph wanted to go out on a date. She was interested in her. Cold, furry paws of fear scampered up her back and a fanatical fluttering in her stomach drove her off the stool.

"Listen," Chris said. "I know you. Don't overthink this. You'd do good by shutting your brain off for once and just being in the moment."

"I've gotta go," she said as she stuffed her phone into a pocket and grabbed her keys. The last time her brain had suddenly become this discombobulated was when she'd been in a 5.5 Richter scale earthquake. But this time, she wasn't shaken from what had just happened but from what was about to happen. Nervous energy raced up and down her arms and legs and she was afraid she'd explode if she didn't start moving them.

She didn't hear what Chris said next or if she'd said anything at all. She swung the bar door open and sprinted out into the last rays of Los Angeles daylight.

❖

Paige didn't have as much time as she'd hoped to get ready for her date.

She shampooed her hair, rinsed, and stepped out of the shower, all the while fighting the silly chant of "I've got a date with Avalon Randolph" that relentlessly resounded in her head.

By the time she was dressed in her fifth choice of outfits, the mantra had died down. Now, the serious business of straightening the house without breaking into a sweat kept her brain busy. If her neighbor had chosen to look through his window, he'd think she'd gone bonkers. She wasted five minutes fixating on the correct arrangement of pillows on the couch. Her motor functions were somehow stuck in that loop, unable to re-engage in another task.

Her nerves were beyond shot, but she finally pulled away

from the cushion madness and poured a quick finger of rye whiskey.

As she tipped the glass and the alcohol shot down her throat, the doorbell suddenly rang. She frantically coughed in surprise, trying to keep the whiskey from reversing direction.

"Hi," Avalon said when Paige opened the door. She looked radiant in a short off-white dress and matching heels. Paige was glad to have picked a tight blue skirt and white blouse because she wasn't over- or under-dressed in comparison.

"Hi. Come in?"

She watched Avalon survey her place, wondering what she thought of it. She had the great fortune to rent an apartment in the North Harper Avenue Historic District, which was one block below the heart of the Sunset Strip. A home in such a quaint and quiet part of West Hollywood was quite a find.

Avalon walked around her place, lightly touching the furniture and taking in the room with the reverence of a visit to a museum.

"The Villa Primavera," Avalon finally said of the apartment building. "This is terrific."

"How did you know?"

"That architecture dream, remember?" Avalon stopped next to the tufted-back Chesterfield sofa. "This building is also called the Hidden Hideaway because the dense landscaping keeps it virtually concealed from the street. And this whole block is on the National Register of Historic Places. During Hollywood's Golden Age, do you know who lived here?"

"Katharine Hepburn and James Dean."

"It's quite a step back in time."

Avalon seemed transfixed, which helped lighten the weight of Paige's anxiety.

"This French parlor-style bronze chandelier, is it original to the apartment?"

"It is, yes."

Paige had fallen in love with the elegant light fixture as soon as she saw it. The entire apartment had a classy but sentimental feel. After researching 1940s interior design, she'd repainted the room in lavender with thin black trim and cleaned every crystal drop hanging from the candelabra-shaped chandelier base.

"Absolutely lovely."

She was sure Avalon heard her relieved exhale but, thankfully, she didn't acknowledge it. Suddenly, it was very important that Avalon like her. She tried to discern whether it was because she was famous or because Paige was attracted to her. Being fascinated with Avalon's celebrity status could overshadow the person she was, so she needed to ignore the former and concentrate on Avalon, the woman.

"Are you ready to go?" Avalon said. "I've made reservations at the Hotel Bel-Air."

This was just a date with a new person, she reminded herself, but her nerves weren't listening. She quickly rubbed a slight layer of dampness from her hands and cursed inwardly for not brushing her teeth again, just in case. Were sweat stains already forming in her armpits? Were her heels high enough to encourage a colossal stumble out on the sidewalk? She cleared her throat to restrain any embarrassing, high-pitched response. "I'll get my purse."

❖

Although it was a very short drive from her apartment, down Sunset Boulevard and north on Stone Canyon Road, Paige had never been to the Hotel Bel-Air. Her hunger usually drove her to Gelson's Market or to one of the many practical ethnic eateries dappled about West Hollywood. She'd never considered frequenting a place that catered almost exclusively to the Hollywood elite.

The valets swiftly and efficiently took Avalon's Mercedes, and Avalon led her through a large tropical garden exploding with the purple blossoms of jacaranda trees and the pink flowers of a huge floss tree. They crossed an arching stone bridge that looked down upon a stream filled with swans so white, they had to have been hand bleached and then placed there to gracefully traverse the waters with effortlessly poised sophistication.

A pink-brick path led them past grand sycamore trees and broad expanses of bougainvillea to a regal dining room whose centerpiece was a roaring fireplace standing guard amid magnificent framed art.

They were shown to a beautiful outdoor Spanish courtyard with quaint booths. In the farthest corner they sat in a very private alcove overlooking a lake inhabited by even more exceedingly refined swans. The maître d' closed the curtains around their alcove, which left them bathed in the sultry glow of a stunning seeded-glass pendant light.

The menu featured an amalgamation of French and Californian cuisine, all touting the best in all-natural, sustainable seafood, poultry, and beef, accompanied by freshly harvested vegetables and fruit.

While Paige could have ordered one of every scrumptious-sounding item on the menu, she picked the seafood salad. Avalon ordered the same, and they waited for dinner by sipping the lemon water that the waiter quickly delivered before he retreated behind the curtain.

"So what made you pick *Cut to the Chase* as the title of this book?" Avalon asked.

"Other than the reference to action scenes, I just like the phrase."

Avalon nodded. "It's become part of our everyday vernacular."

"Do you know how it came about?"

Avalon shook her head. "I know it comes from the movies, but strangely, it's never used on the set."

"In the 1920s, the formula of many of the silent films had obligatory romantic story lines, but they always ended them in chase sequences. The first reference I found in my research came from a script direction for a movie based on the novel *Hollywood Girl*. It said something like, 'Jannings escapes…cut to chase.' It became popular later when an article about screenwriting came out. Helen Deutsch—"

"Helen Deutsch who wrote *National Velvet*?"

She was relieved that her diatribe was at least holding Avalon's attention. "Yes. Helen had a note on the wall where she did her writing. Time was important to her because it said, 'When in doubt, cut to the chase.'"

"So, cut to the chase by cutting to the chase."

She hadn't heard it put that way and laughed. "Yes."

Avalon bent slightly forward. "Are you the kind that likes to get to the point?"

She wasn't sure what that meant and couldn't tell by the look in Avalon's eyes if it was a simple question or a double entendre. The fact that her mind went there made her quickly scold herself. Yes, they were on a date, but they hadn't even been served their dinner rolls yet.

"I suppose," she said, "I don't beat around the bush…" She suddenly flushed at what could be misconstrued as another innuendo. "I mean, I usually get to the point, yes." As embarrassed as if she had just spilled ketchup on her boobs, she quickly took a drink of her water.

"I would imagine you do." Avalon's expression was adorable and she regarded her with what looked like amusement.

"What about you?" She resorted to obvious subterfuge, but she was going to choke on her water if she didn't redirect the conversation.

"Do I get to the point?" Avalon's amusement lingered in her half smile. "Too often, sometimes. I'm not known for my shyness."

"Have you always been that way or do you think Hollywood changed you?"

"I suppose a little of both. You can be the most outgoing, self-assured person, but this industry has a way of hypnotizing you with a spell that can threaten your ego. It can certainly activate the dark and dangerous side in all of us."

"Do you think everyone has a dark and dangerous side?"

"I didn't used to think so." Her face changed as she sat back and looked skyward a moment. "I was eighteen when I first moved here, the stereotypical girl just off the bus from Indiana. I had read in some old Hollywood book about all the superstitions that actors believe in order to get famous or remain famous. So the first thing I tried was the one that seemed the most magical. I went to the corner of Hollywood Boulevard and Vine Street and found the five stars they mentioned in the book—the ones of Katharine Hepburn, Gene Autry, Mary Pickford, Douglas Fairbanks, and Cecil B. DeMille. At each of the stars, I walked around it five times, counterclockwise, and stopped where I could look down and read the name on it.

"Then I said three times, 'I want to be a great star, will you be my friend,' bent down, and patted each point of the star saying, 'Thank you.'

"I'd read that if the spirits liked me, I'd become a big star and never have any problems in Hollywood. The book said 'if,' because if I hadn't asked with sincerity, these same spirits would have driven me out of Hollywood permanently."

"You actually did that?"

"I did."

"It looks like they all became your friends."

"It was a little silly," Avalon said, "but at the time I believed it with all my heart. I look back on that and I know I've changed from that first day. Hollywood pushes you to be perfect and shoves challenges and temptation in your face. All that stress makes you change and you find out about your dark side. I guess that's why this town relies on silly little superstitions."

"People need protection from the bad, I suppose. Like, you're never supposed to say the name of a play backstage and you never wish anyone good luck."

"Break a leg."

"Exactly. You never bring peanuts backstage and, of course, you never, ever whistle there either."

"Carmen Diaz says she knocks on wood all day long."

"And I heard," Paige said, "that Lady Gaga won't have casual sex with people because she thinks it will steal her creativity."

"Wow." Avalon's eyebrows rose. "I didn't know that creativity comes from the vagina." She made a face that looked like she'd seen an alien and stared down at her lap.

Paige laughed out loud. "That's why she's at the top of the charts."

"She's very smart, that one."

They both laughed and a wave of calmness washed over Paige. She was beginning to forget who she was dining with.

Dinner was perfect, and just as they were finishing, the waiter brought them two glasses of rosolio as their digestif, explaining that the liqueur, invented by a fourteenth-century Catholic doctor and infused with rose petals and lavender, was with compliments from the management.

As they waited for the Hotel Bel-Air valet to bring Avalon's car around, Avalon slipped her arm into Paige's.

"Would you like to go to my house?"

She stopped a moment to think. Did that mean more B movies or something much more…involved? Was she ready for that? She'd never slept with a woman on a first date. Was that what she meant? Was Avalon looking for a one-night stand?

"Ahhh…" She hated sounding so indecisive, but suddenly she was dreadfully nervous. Was it okay if they just *did it*? She was a grown woman who could make any choices she wanted. And what would be the harm? She was lucky enough to have been invited out by Avalon. That was the most exciting thing that had happened to her in ages. Still, she felt uncertain and inhibited.

"Sure," she said, with as much confidence and nonchalance as she could muster.

She couldn't relax, though, as they drove away from the restaurant. Visions of sex swings, phallic toys, and rubber items flew around her mind. An actress as wild as Avalon was reported to be must take delightful pleasure in devouring her conquests. Would there be any romantic foreplay? Would a video camera be involved? Had Paige shaved everywhere?

She was so caught up running sexual scenarios in her mind that, a block later, she almost didn't notice that they'd turned east on Hollywood Boulevard.

"We're heading away from your house."

"Uh-huh," Avalon said.

"We're not going to the Palisades?"

Avalon put a hand to her mouth and chuckled. "Oh! I'm sorry. We're not going to my house. We're going to My House. It's a club in Hollywood."

"Oh." Paige wanted to fold herself into her purse and snap it shut. She turned away, hoping Avalon didn't see the way her cheeks burned. She was sure they looked like ripe tomatoes.

"I need to tell you something," Avalon said. "There's that whole intrusive thing with the paparazzi. They're always there, so I hope you're okay with that."

She nodded.

"Just stay close to me and the bar security will help us."

They pulled up to the curb and Paige watched a throng of casually dressed people milling about, as well as a fairly long line of others in swankier attire behind roped-off stanchions. Two valet attendants opened their doors. In the time it took Paige to exit the passenger side of the car and step onto the sidewalk, a throng of photographers had surrounded Avalon. Paige stepped toward her and instinctively grabbed her arm, pulling her close. The assault of cameras thrust in their faces and questions yelled at high volume was furious and fanatical.

In the middle of the cacophony, her grip slipped from Avalon's arm and she stepped on someone's shoe. Among the shouting, she heard some of the same questions from the day on Selma Street.

"Avalon, where's Jessica?"

"Any more parties at Club Raunch?"

Avalon reached out and grabbed her hand just as two security men in black suits pushed their way through the crowd.

"Who's your date, Avalon?"

"Certainly not Jessica," Avalon said, and the paparazzi seemed to move in even tighter.

The only time Paige had ever felt this smashed in and claustrophobic was on her first and only New York subway ride. And it was just as unpleasant.

As the security guards encircled her and Avalon, moving them toward the door of the club, one voice punched through the rest.

"Jessica's back in town. Did you know that, Avalon?"

Avalon's hand tightened around Paige's. She couldn't see her face but apparently the question had hit a nerve. However, this time she said nothing more and they walked inside.

My House was mind-boggling in its directness. Taken literally, the interior looked like someone's private, but very glamorous, home. Paige took in the rooms, both classical and contemporary and satiated with textures and architectural details. There was a dining room, a grand staircase that led to a second floor, and a view out to a backyard with an impressive-looking barbeque. The kitchen, replete with marble counters and dark wood cabinets, served as the main bar. From there, the smell of freshly baked cookies wafted unexpectedly toward her.

Avalon took her through the ultrachic crowd that, she swore, smelled not of cookies, but of the posh aroma of money.

They sat on a velvet sofa in the sunken living room. Paige had to reach out and touch the alligator-hide coffee tables to see if they were real. In keeping with the trendy green and socially conscious ethos of Hollywood, they were faux.

Drinks came, as well as more people than Paige could count. Avalon talked to them all, but it was obvious that she was trying to be as short as possible with them.

Finally, Avalon said, "This place isn't going to allow us to talk. Would you like to go somewhere else?"

As they left, the same crowd of jean-clad cameramen surrounded the security guards who escorted her and Avalon, but this time she didn't talk to any of them.

In the car, Avalon apologized for the quick exit.

"I imagine that happens a lot," Paige said as they headed west on Hollywood Boulevard.

"Yeah. Try shopping for shoes on Melrose. Even getting a late-night hankering for Häagen-Dazs incites a small mob. Those guys are everywhere. I think they radio each other because they turn up at the strangest places. Funny thing is, they pretty much leave me alone at my house."

After her partial meltdown earlier, she debated a moment. Before, when she thought "my house" was Avalon's place, it had shocked her. But she was a grown woman and could edit her own principles. Did she even have principles in a first-date situation like this? And it was only a first date. Ah, hell, she thought. "Do you want to go there?"

Avalon turned to look at her a moment. "Sure."

She couldn't tell from Avalon's response whether she was waiting for that question or not, but it didn't matter. As Avalon sped back down Hollywood Boulevard, Paige took a deep breath. She was nervous about the possible consequences of her question. It was only a heartbeat ago that she'd left Avalon's house after their movie night, feeling lucky to have dodged a big bullet of potential disappointment. If Avalon was just looking for some fun, Paige could be dumped right after, and that would hurt.

She realized she was anxiously jiggling her foot back and forth and stopped. An old college psychology class came to mind. She remembered Gestalt therapist Fritz Perls asking a client, "Your foot is shaking, what is your foot saying right now?"

Well, her foot was saying, "I'm getting ready to run the minute I feel she's just using me for her own amusement." And if the question was supposed to heighten her body awareness, she'd have to add that her stomach was a Keno cage of tumbling numbered balls and her shaking hands might as well have just arrived from a winter in Alaska.

She clasped her hands together to calm them.

Yes, this was a first date, she reasoned, and maybe a last date. What was so bad about that? She was here, wasn't she? And whatever happened was better than not being with Avalon at all.

That logic might not hold up, but as she pushed her clenched hands into her stomach, to slow down the tumbling Keno balls, she decided she'd try to relax and just enjoy the evening.

CHAPTER TEN

A valon deactivated a very elaborate alarm system while Paige stood by the bay window. The street had few lampposts and was very dark, and she wondered why until she realized there was a reason for that design decision. Out the large bay window, the moon's reflection shimmered on the water like a million amber fireflies floating in a magical line from the horizon to the shore.

She stepped in and, just as Avalon turned some lights on, Avalon's cell phone rang. As Paige turned away from the view, she saw Avalon turn the cell phone off and drop it on the coffee table.

"I've got water, some hard stuff, wine…"

"Red?"

"Merlot?"

"Sure."

She followed Avalon into the kitchen.

"So, you were born in Indiana?"

Avalon retrieved two glasses from a cupboard and a bottle from an elaborately carved wine rack on the counter. "Yup. I wasn't kidding when I said I was that girl fresh off the bus."

"Who's at home?"

"My mom. I'm an only child. My dad died when I was seven. So it was just me and her." She poured two glasses of dark scarlet wine and gave one to Paige. "My mom was one of those triple-P types."

"Triple-P?"

"Popular and perfectly poised. She drilled that into me, too. I was her main focus, even before Dad died. Sometimes I think that focus somehow caused my dad's death. He was always kind of a third wheel. I don't even remember much of him." She took a sip. "I was the center of my mom's world, like a sculpture she was chiseling away at, night and day. And I lived for her spotlight, no matter how hard it was to dwell in the triple Ps. I mean, I love her, but it was so hard to be her daughter."

She rested against the counter by the sink, a few feet away from Paige. "What about you? Where were you born?"

"Here in Los Angeles. Never left."

"A native Californian? That's as rare as rocking-horse poop." Avalon paused. "I'm sorry, I didn't mean you were poop. It's just that I haven't met many real California-born people in LA."

Paige laughed. "I know what you mean. It seems like everyone who's born here leaves to make room for all your Indiana buses."

Avalon laughed. "Touché."

"I have two brothers who live here, as well. And my parents are still in the same house."

"That's really nice."

She shrugged. "I suppose. But the truth is, everyone in my family is an accomplished academic in the university system. They're not too keen on what I write."

"You mean they think textbooks are the only true forms of literature?"

"Yeah. My mom calls my work soft literature. My brother calls it picture books. I mean, I guess they are, but it's just the way they say it."

"But you're successful, so what do they say to that?"

"The same thing they'd say about anyone who didn't pursue

a career in line with their college degree. That I'm wasting my life. It was a travesty that my BS took a backseat to my liberal-arts interest."

"Well, I never went to college, so I'd for sure be a boundless dinnertime topic of conversation." Avalon refilled their glasses and then reached for her hand. "Come here."

Avalon led her to the couch and as they sat she said, "So, who encourages your work?"

"My best friend, Chris. She's proud of me, and that makes up for a lot."

"It's important to have a support system. There are too many naysayers out there and it's hard not to listen to them. Especially if they're related to you. What about you? Who's the most important person in your life?" She imagined there were a million fans who reminded her every day that she was loved.

Avalon didn't answer right away. She blinked a few times and her face seemed to be frozen. The look of vulnerability or uncertainty struck Paige hard. She felt the thudding pang of concern in her heart.

Then, like a September snowfall, Avalon's smile came a little too quickly. "My agent and my manager. I confide in Tawnya the most. And," she laughed, "the most important person in my life is the next producer who will hire me."

When Avalon had appeared to be searching for a response, Paige wasn't sure whether she was picking one person of many or choosing the right answer. It stunned her that Avalon seemed to be struggling for any answer.

"Tell me about Chris." Avalon had changed the topic.

"She's a K9 police officer with a beautiful dog named Abel. We live fairly close to each other and we've been friends forever, it seems. She's more down-to-earth than anyone I know."

"Were you two ever…"

"Together? No. I never seem to fall in love with my friends and never seem to like my lovers."

"Yeah, why is that? I think my lovers end up hating me with as much passion as they loved me."

"Opposite and equal forces, I suppose."

"How long has it been since your last relationship?"

"Not long enough. Marlene and I broke up about three months ago, but the way she still finds me to bitch about me makes it seem like we're still together."

"What does she have to bitch about?"

Paige counted off on her fingers. "I was always working. I'm boring. And I'm not good in bed. Oh, my God, did I just say that?"

"No. She said that."

"I'm so embarrassed."

"Don't be." Avalon placed her fingers on Paige's knee. "Tell her to fuck off."

The gesture stirred together a strong brew of comfort and nervousness. "Oh, that would be something you could do. I…I'm not like that."

"Mean?"

"No! Just bold and in-your-face. Sometimes I wish I could be."

"Hand me your phone."

"What?"

"Hand me your phone. Let's call her and tell her right now."

"No!"

"It could be liberating."

Paige raised her wineglass. "I'd need a few more of these. But then I still don't think I could do that."

"Well," Avalon said, "I've said it to my ex a few hundred times, but she hasn't gotten the message. Maybe it's not as liberating as I thought."

"That photographer said that Jessica was back in town." Paige hesitated because she might be prying.

"If you want to know where the gay bars are in a new town, ask a taxi driver. If you want to know where your ex is, ask a stalkarazzi."

"Did it bother you?"

"A little bit. She won't accept that we're done. It was a relief when she went out of state on vacation."

"Hand me your phone."

Avalon paused and then laughed so genuinely that Paige's nervousness calmed.

"I think we should introduce our exes," Paige said. "That way, they can go off and torment each other."

"Okay. Enough about exes. It's not a good subject for a first date."

"Agreed."

"How's the book going?"

"Very well, actually. I've got a crazy deadline so it's upped the ante, but I think I'll make it."

Avalon didn't reply but her expression softened quite a bit, and Paige relaxed. In the silence, she regarded her, wondering what her life was really like. Did she have trouble finding people who saw her for her? It was hard to trust in a town that was often devious and corrupt.

Avalon edged closer. It seemed, at that moment, that Hollywood was very far from Avalon's mind. "You're beautiful."

Paige took in a breath and held it. Their faces were inches apart and a quiver of excitement buzzed in her ears. It seemed too silly to tell her she was beautiful, too, so she kept looking into her eyes without saying anything. The moon glowed through the bay window, casting Avalon in a honey-colored luminosity.

"You're a unique woman," Avalon said. "Different from the ones I've met."

The moment was surreal. Paige's brain tried to collect and analyze the thoughts she was having but just couldn't. Chris had told her not to overthink and to shut her brain off. It was a scary move for her, but she surrendered the mental effort. More than anything, she wanted to just feel.

She didn't register any sounds, no waves crashing on the beach below or cars passing by. The silence itself rang loudly in her ears. She felt the pulse in her neck increase when the sweet and spicy aroma of Avalon's perfume drifted toward her.

Avalon inched even closer. With the gentleness that the seeds of a dandelion globe float through the air, their lips met. Her mouth was sexy and yielding, and Paige felt dizzy with sudden bliss. At first, she just responded, letting Avalon take the lead, but her desire grew quickly. She cupped the back of Avalon's head in her hand and their mouths opened in unison, tongues gently exploring and tasting.

Somewhere in the distant alcoves of her logic, a voice of caution rose, warning her of the consequences of where this first date was going. She fought the urge to slow the pace. Avalon certainly wasn't throwing her down on the couch so she reminded herself to just…stop…thinking.

They kissed for a long time, and then Avalon moaned softly and took Paige's hand. She guided her off the couch, and into her bedroom.

When they got to the bed, Avalon unzipped Paige's skirt and unbuttoned her blouse, letting them fall about their feet. As Avalon undressed, slowly revealing her breasts, stomach, and legs, the sight transfixed Paige.

She'd never forget the first time their warm, exposed skin met as they embraced. Breast against breast, hips against hips, they stood together, kissing in the darkened room. Avalon's nipples hardened against hers and Paige's breath quickened.

A gentle push from Avalon landed them on the bed, side by side. Their kissing grew more intense, and when Avalon wrapped her leg over Paige, pushing her hips into her, Paige's excitement skyrocketed as if the fuse of a one-ton Roman candle had just hit its ignition point.

She moved on top, growing wetter as Avalon's obvious agreement came out as a moan.

"You fit so well," Avalon said, "right here, between my legs."

As Paige pushed against her, she felt Avalon's wetness and went weak inside. Raw desire seized her as they kissed. The exquisite raking of Avalon's nails down her back made her arch up and coaxed her to follow the path downward. Jolts of electricity spread from her stomach like hot currents of desire and craving, searching for a circuit to blow. And when she moved downward, kissing a path to Avalon's hips, she longed to let her fingers and mouth be the instruments to express those hot rushes of raw need.

Avalon opened her legs and lifted her head, holding Paige's in her hands. She brushed the hair from her eyes. Paige paused briefly before tasting the woman who was driving her crazy. Avalon laid her head back, moaning slightly as her body undulated under her. She was slick with velvety wetness and Paige slipped two fingers inside her, coaxing little gasps from Avalon as she found the tight band of her G-spot.

Avalon lifted her head again and their eyes locked. The desire to please her, to be part of her in that moment, pounded against her chest. She found where Avalon was the most sensitive and swirled her tongue lightly, slowly. Avalon's eyelashes dipped but she kept her eyes open. A dreamy half smile formed on her lips before she licked it away with her tongue and moaned.

Avalon's breathing quickened and her hips moved faster so Paige slowed down, wanting the feeling to last.

"Don't stop, please," Avalon murmured, almost desperately.

Paige learned, in just a short moment, exactly what Avalon needed. And they were one in their desire to visit that same place of ecstasy and depth. Suddenly, Avalon's body opened up and her orgasm gripped Paige's fingers. Their eyes met again and Paige matched Avalon's bucking hips with strokes of her tongue. As

Avalon came, her eyes showed her the depth of her soul. Paige's heart wanted to burst because Avalon was letting her into the deepest place inside her. And even after her moans started to quiet, Paige, her chin slick with Avalon's wetness, didn't want to stop.

Avalon's body began to slowly relax as little shivers erupted, rippling her stomach muscles. Paige tried to slow her breathing, her heartbeat, but she could still feel Avalon gripping her fingers in smaller waves.

She eventually pulled her fingers from Avalon and made her way up into her arms.

Wet with sweat and with Avalon's excitement, she exhaled, melting into her and relaxing to her touch.

"Kiss me," Avalon said as she wrapped her arms around Paige, holding her so lovingly.

In that moment, she felt safe and happy. Avalon stroked her hair with feathery-light fingertips and kissed her forehead.

"Oh, my God," Avalon whispered, and when she cleared her throat, a tear dropped onto Paige's cheek.

Paige raised up, gently catching more with the back of her hand. "Are you okay?"

"Yeah," she said. "It's just that…it was so intense." Avalon hugged her tight, and Paige held on as if she might fly away. Avalon's lovemaking had satiated her body, but her emotions quickly swelled.

She closed her eyes, letting Avalon's heartbeat soothe her.

"Marlene is dead wrong about you in bed," Avalon finally said.

Paige chuckled and kissed her neck, but Avalon broke the kiss by pushing her over onto her back.

"We're not done yet," she said as she looked down on her with a grin so sexy, Paige felt her heart falling into the deep seas of passion. She imagined how incredible this kind of drowning would feel. They were together in an ocean that Avalon had created, and the waves were growing so immense, she knew she would soon be overcome by her feelings for her.

Whether they made love again or just held each other, she certainly wouldn't get any sleep tonight.

CHAPTER ELEVEN

Paige awoke to the squeal and wheeze of the street sweeper outside her apartment. When the quiet returned, recollections of the night before came slowly into focus and then, more clearly, the almost implausible memories of Avalon's body tangled in hers.

Avalon Randolph. Was it possible?

The weight of a more pressing question, however, fell heavily on her chest. Had it been a one-night stand? When Avalon had driven her home, they'd hugged and Avalon held her for the longest time. And she'd waited until Paige was safely inside her courtyard before driving away. She sighed, knowing she couldn't draw any conclusions from those gestures.

Her cell phone rang and she grabbed it, hoping it was Avalon.

"What's this I'm watching on TV, Paige?"

It was her mother. "I don't know," she said, rubbing her eyes and not caring to hide the disappointment in her voice.

"On this show about actors and entertainment, you're going into some club or something with Avalon Randolph. Are you seeing Avalon Randolph?"

"I don't know if you'd call it that."

"Well, what is it?"

Why did she need to know? She hadn't called when her first two books were published, but for this she had to pick up the phone?

"We went out, Mom. Why are you concerned?"

"I'm not concerned. Just surprised, I suppose."

"Surprised by what?" That a celebrity would be interested in her? That she was on television?

"It just seems a bit salacious."

There it was. The always-proper mother worried that her daughter would do something to embarrass the highly intellectual and practical family.

"You don't need to worry about me, Mom." She wasn't her mother's true worry, but maybe a little passive aggression might get across to her.

"That's not it."

Or maybe not. Paige sighed. This wasn't the way she wanted to wake up. "Okay. What bothers you about this?"

"That lifestyle, Paige. We all know what it does to people."

"And what is that, Mom?" She had no desire to make it easy for her.

"Parties, alcohol, drugs—"

"If I suddenly decide to become a drug addict, I'll let you know. But for now, I need to get up and get some work done."

"You're being flip, aren't you?"

"I'm telling you not to be upset. I gotta go."

She said good-bye and rolled out of bed, wincing as she stood. Her hip and groin muscles protested, sending throbbing reminders of their recent workout. It had been a while since she'd enjoyed that kind of exercise, and it was painfully obvious that she'd found herself in more innovative positions than she'd ever known existed.

She felt the weight of no sleep, and it took a few seconds longer to collect her thoughts and figure out what day it was and what she was supposed to do.

A shower and a cup of coffee would help, but before she could make it to the bathroom, her doorbell rang.

"You off today?" Chris walked through the door Paige held open and plopped down on her couch. She was in blue board shorts, a white T-shirt, and flip-flops.

"No, but it looks like you are."

"I'm here to persuade you to go to Venice Beach. It's beautiful out," she said as she examined her arms, "and I'm getting a bit pasty."

Paige shuffled toward the kitchen, favoring her tender quadriceps as they had now joined the silent protest.

"Hey," Chris said, "you look like you were rolled in an alley."

"I was on a date." Why wasn't the coffee dripping faster?

Chris charged into the kitchen so fast she startled Paige's already slow-functioning brain.

"My God! Don't do that!"

"Your date with Avalon!"

She nodded, frustrated that the caffeine might as well have been molasses the way it seeped from the filter.

"You...she...you two...?"

Paige was still trying to sort it out herself. She turned to Chris, who was crouched in a football stance, looking like she was ready to receive a hiked ball. Her hands were out in front of her, but they were gesturing to the area below Paige's waistline.

Paige slapped her hands away. "What are you doing?"

"You...her...you two...?"

"You already said that."

Chris cuffed her hands to her head. She was now beginning to look like one of the Three Stooges. "How can you sit there making coffee like last night was no big deal?"

"Last night was a big deal. I'm just trying to process it." Thankfully, her cup was finally full. She took it back to the couch as Chris shadowed her.

"Okay," Chris said, jumping on the couch and crossing her legs, Indian style, as if settling in for a fireside story, "tell me what happened."

She recounted the date, telling her about the nice dinner and the exciting spectacle she'd experienced at the club. Maybe it was her lack of sleep, but it was as if she were describing someone else's night. She felt out of her body and a little overwhelmed.

"And then what?" Chris seemed transfixed.

Paige got up to refill her coffee.

From the couch, Chris said, "Did you…?"

"Yes, we did."

Chris looked toward the bedroom as if ethereal remnants of Avalon and her were still visible.

"Not there. We went to her place."

"How was it?"

She rested her hip against the counter and rubbed her eyes, still swimming in the feel of Avalon's body. A jolt of exhilaration erupted inside her as she recalled the way Avalon had stared into her eyes when she came. She'd never experienced that before. The connection they'd made was complete and absolute.

"It was…amazing."

"Wow." Chris paused, then said, "So why do you look like the ice cream just fell off your cone?"

She picked up her coffee mug and returned to the couch. "I'm just blown away, I guess. I mean, I've never had sex with someone this quickly."

Chris stared at her like a child who'd just seen a picture of boobies. "You had sex with Avalon."

"Yeah. And I don't know what it means. I don't know if it was a one-night stand or not."

"You like her."

"I do," she said slowly.

"Then just see what happens." Chris patted her knee. "You had an extraordinary night, and who knows? Maybe you'll be the next Ms. Randolph."

"I don't want to go there, Chris."

"Look, everything will work out fine. And you should get some sleep. You look like death warmed over."

"I was headed to the shower when you came by."

"So, do you wanna go to Venice Beach? You could get some shut-eye on the sand."

She had to sort through the photos and write some text, but the way her head felt, she wasn't sure she'd make much sense of anything. Avalon wasn't filming that day so she didn't have any set work to catch. Her phone rang. She spoke into it and then mouthed to Chris, "It's Dee Jae.

"Hi, Deej. What are you up to?"

Chris pointed to the phone, shaking her finger. "Ask her if she wants to go."

"Chris wants to know if you want to go to Venice Beach with us. Yeah. In an hour?"

She hung up and said, "Okay. Just give me a few to shower and change."

Chris reclined back on the couch. "I'll be right here, imagining Avalon and you. Well, not you, you're my best friend. I'll just sit here and think about Avalon."

"You need a checkup from the neck up." Paige pushed off the couch and headed toward the bathroom. But she knew Chris wasn't the only one who would be thinking about Avalon. She opened the shower nozzles to full blast, and when she disrobed, she turned toward the mirror. Her body didn't look any different than it had the night before, but her insides had been altered significantly.

A shiver of vulnerability vibrated throughout her body. She'd slept with Avalon. No, more than slept with her. She'd made love to her.

She'd opened the door to a level of pleasure and intensity she never thought possible. It penetrated so deeply into her soul and psyche that she considered slamming the door shut before she got hurt. But doing that now, after she'd shared a bed with

Avalon, was as difficult as trying to shove a bullet back into a fired gun.

❖

Dee Jae waved to Paige and Chris as they stepped onto the sand at the junction of Wave Crest Avenue and Ocean Front Walk. Venice Beach was fairly crowded, as it usually was, but they found a nice area away from some of the more bizarre overly tan musclemen, transvestites on roller skates, and homeless people in Hawaiian shirts.

Paige and Chris hugged Dee Jae and set up their beach chairs.

"You smell like summer," Paige said as she and Chris peeled off their shorts and shirt.

"Coconut and piña colada," Dee Jae said as she handed her a bottle of lotion. She wore a sundress to hide what she said was her plumpness, but Paige thought she was beautiful. They'd met when Paige attended a play that Dee Jae produced. She was the head of a women's theater company in Hollywood, and their friendship had developed immediately. Any time she needed framed pictures for props, Paige happily supplied them.

Paige adjusted her bikini, sloshed some sunscreen on her arms and legs, and handed it to Chris. "How are things at the theater?"

"Going well. We go dark next month and I teach a writing workshop after that."

"What's your next play?"

"I'm considering a few but haven't found anything that really strikes me, you know? Maybe something will come from the workshop. At the end I'm producing a showcase for my students' writing."

Chris handed the lotion back to Dee Jae. "Ask Paige who she's dating."

"Chris, geez."

"Who?"

Paige shook her head and then slouched back in the chair.

"Avalon Randolph," Chris said.

Dee Jae slapped Paige's stomach, the soggy sound of the lotion smacking loudly.

"Ouch."

"You star fucker, you."

"Dee Jae!"

"I'm just kidding," Dee Jae said. She looked at Chris. "But are you kidding?"

Chris shook her head, grinning like a maniac.

Paige moaned. "No, but I wouldn't call it dating."

"Tell me all about it!"

Paige stood and moved her chair to the side. She straightened out her beach towel and lay facedown. "I'm going to take a nap, ladies."

As she closed her eyes and felt the tiredness pulling at her brain, she heard Chris say, "Well, I'll tell you about it."

"No, you won't." Paige's voice was muffled from the towel but she knew her words were clear enough.

There was a pause and then she heard Chris whisper, "Avalon...*fuckin' A!*"

"That's enough, Officer Bergstrom." She still hadn't shaken the vulnerability she felt. She didn't want to hear Chris go on about Avalon until she could have more time to sort through her feelings.

Avalon unzipped the fifth dress that had been handed to her. She was in the wardrobe department at the studio, getting alterations on the clothing she was supposed to wear for upcoming scenes. Two wardrobe assistants measured and pinned while she stepped in and out of a curtained-off area near the sewing machines.

Michele D. had arrived right after Avalon but had spent half the time on her cell phone and the other just watching them work. A brooding cloud seemed to be hovering over her frowning face.

One assistant took the dress from Avalon while the other searched for the next.

"What's with you, Michele?" Avalon finally said. "Did you accidentally sit on your gold-plated Montblanc?"

"Funny."

"What is it?"

"As your manager—"

"Wait a minute. Every time you start with 'as your manager,' you end up telling me something's for my own good. And it usually isn't."

"I simply saw the way you were interacting with Paige."

Avalon bristled at her tone. "And?"

"Come on, I know you, Avalon. She'll be in your bed before the light at Hollywood and Vine turns green."

"What the fuck is wrong with you?" She felt the hot flare of infuriation ignite her cheeks. "You've been on my ass since I broke up with Jessica. I'm single now and it's nobody's business what I do."

"In case you forgot, which it seems you did, it *is* my business." She put her hand on her hip, which made Avalon roll her eyes. "You put me in charge of plotting the course that leads you toward your ultimate goal, which is to become Hollywood's highest-paid actor. Remember that? I know exactly who you are. I know your strengths and weaknesses. And women are one of your weaknesses."

If she had wondered whether to tell Michele D. about the night before, she had her answer. "That mess with Jessica is yesterday's news."

"It's still news, Avalon. The press is following you and Jessica around everywhere you go. They're looking for any dirty laundry they can find. Your breakup did some heavy damage and you can't afford any more crap like that."

"So I'm supposed to become a nun? Jesus, Michele, dating is part of life."

"And your life happens to be scrutinized every time you step outside. Do you know what I had to do to calm the producers down? They already think you're unpredictable. Listen, I'm your advisor. I invest considerable time and money in your career, and I'm the one who gets you waived from going to the auditions that everyone else has to. But any more of this stuff and you'll be back to begging for roles, Avalon. I'm warning you that you'll go off the rails again if you get all wrapped up in the photographer."

Gladys returned with a pantsuit and Avalon grabbed it. "This town doesn't own me, Michele. Remember that."

Avalon shut her out with a swipe of the curtain and listened while Michele turned on an expensive heel and clopped out of the wardrobe room.

Her cell phone began to play Israel "Iz" Kamakawiwo'ole's version of "Somewhere Over the Rainbow." It was the ringtone she'd selected for her mother.

"Hi, Mom."

"Avalon." She sounded so tired. "Are you doing all right, darling?"

"I'm fine. Why?"

"I watch the TV and I worry." There wasn't much else to do in that dead little town in Indiana. Avalon had tried to convince her to move to Los Angeles once, but she insisted on staying. At least there she could make a few dollars teaching etiquette to grade-school girls. It seemed that after Avalon moved to Hollywood, her mother needed others to mold into popular-and-perfectly-poised little people. Now that she had a famous daughter, other

LISA GIROLAMI

mothers would send their girls to her. It was a chance to get out of the Midwest, she supposed.

"I told you all of that is just BS. They only show the bad stuff."

"There seems to be a lot of it lately."

"I'm really okay. How are you?"

"It gets harder every day. The economy is pretty bad."

"Do you need some money?"

"I hate to ask…"

"I'll send you some, so don't worry." She'd been a stern mother and tried unsuccessfully to tame her tempestuous daughter, but Avalon knew she always had a vast amount of love at her core.

"Are you in trouble at all?"

"No, Mom."

"Will you come home to visit soon?"

"I'll try, okay?"

"Thank you, dear. For the money."

When she hung up, a substantial weight hung in Avalon's chest. Her mother wanted her to be so perfect. She'd ridden her constantly, watching her and redirecting her even when she ate dinner or watched a little TV. But as unyielding as the strict parenting had been during childhood, her mother seemed almost meek now. Maybe that's why she railed against Michele D. so often. Just her approach, the way she clomped up to Avalon like an old schoolmarm to a high-spirited student, rankled her because she knew she was going to get some kind of admonishment. Of course, Michele D.'s motivation was cemented purely in business; it was her job to control Avalon's world, for Avalon's benefit, but it made her feel like a little child. She wondered if she rebelled because Michele D. reminded her of her mother and the frustration she'd experienced under such a relentlessly stern upbringing. But then again, maybe Michele D. annoyed her and made her sad because she reminded her of the strength and unwavering nature her mother had lost long ago.

• 124 •

And maybe part of what eventually broke her mother's resolve had been Avalon's constant opposition and insurrection. Nothing ever came easily at home; a fight erupted with every procedure or command. And when Avalon ultimately broke away from that world by leaving for Hollywood, she'd clearly been responding to that authoritarian world. It made sense that she'd depleted her mother's strength and that the constant combat had rendered her mother weak and compliant.

She looked at her phone, now dead and disconnected from the woman who'd tried so hard to raise her well. Had she sucked the life force right out of her mother?

With every phone call from her, usually preceded by a TV show or magazine that mentioned her daughter, Avalon felt as if she were letting her mother down. While she'd satisfied the popular part of her rearing, the media didn't often, if ever, portray her as a perfectly poised young lady.

Maybe she had lost herself along the way.

One of the assistants spoke from the other side of the curtain. "How is the pantsuit? May we see?"

Avalon put her cell phone back on the chair and took a deep breath. *Don't be sad*, she told herself. Maybe she wasn't perfectly poised, but she'd gotten the other half right. It was a slim defense, but she'd cling to it.

She shook her head, trying to clear her sorrow, and stepped out from behind the curtain.

❖

"Your cell phone is ringing."

Paige was still facedown on a towel on the sand of Venice Beach, waking from the odd slumber that the hot sun and no sleep had plunged her into. She lifted her head. Dee Jae was asleep.

"Huh?"

Chris pointed to her bag. "Your phone."

She pulled it out. "Hello?"

"I want to see you again." It was Avalon.

"You do? I mean, yes, I'd like that."

"Are you interested in a party tonight? There's a charity event at the Abbey."

She hadn't been to the trendy West Hollywood gay bar in ages. "Sure. What time?"

"I'll pick you up at ten."

She'd forgotten that partiers started later than usual. That would give her time to soak her head in the shower, take a nap, and do some work. "That'd be great."

"And, Paige?"

"Yes?"

"Last night was wonderful."

She needed to hear that. "It was."

"See you tonight."

She hung up and rolled over on her back. There were no clouds in the sky, something at which she shouldn't have been surprised but somehow was. Avalon's call had been a relief. It seemed that the night before hadn't been a one-night stand, but a prickle of apprehension still niggled in the back of her brain. Avalon was beyond what she was used to in women. She was standing at the top of an advanced diamond ski run when she was more comfortable on the bunny slope.

"Was that Avalon?" Dee Jae said.

She put the phone away. "I thought you were asleep."

Chris nodded like a bobblehead doll, her prediction now confirmed. "So, it wasn't a one-night stand."

"I guess not."

"Damn, woman." Chris took off her sunglasses and pointed them at her. "I'd be hollering from the top of the Capitol Records building if I were you. Avalon is calling you—for another *date*. It's like you dropped a penny into the well and a million bucks came flying back up."

"This pace…it's not what I'm used to. I like things a bit more steady and normal."

"You're predictable to a fault, my friend."

Paige's sigh fluttered fretfully in her throat. She had a feeling *predictable* wouldn't be an adjective to describe her upcoming date.

CHAPTER TWELVE

Paige and Avalon walked through the wrought-iron gates of the Abbey. Sitting on Roberson, just south of Santa Monica Boulevard, the bar had a reputation for encouraging everyone who went there to replace all their inhibitions with an attitude as open-minded as its open-air ambience.

They walked through the Cabana bar, lit with seemingly hundreds of candles set on iron holders and shelves, and ordered French Connections at the newer Effen Smooth bar. The dance floor was already full of bodies moving in stuttering flashes under manic strobe lights.

Paige was aware that everyone knew who Avalon was, but in the typical cooler-than-cool Hollywood fashion, they kept their eyes averted, blasé in their concentration.

Avalon kept her close. She held her hand and they snuggled romantically throughout the night.

She was glad to have worn an outfit that matched Avalon's in style, but they would have blended in just as well if they'd worn holey jeans and tank tops. The crowd was dressed in a mix of everything that could be purchased on trendy Melrose Avenue.

Three acquaintances of Avalon's came by, and though Avalon introduced them, it was hard to hear their names. Paige didn't consider herself a complete fuddy-duddy, but she'd never understood the appeal of such noise-inflicted conversation. When

Avalon would put her lips to Paige's ear, she could hear fine, but otherwise she only partially followed the dialogue. Thankfully, the tallest of Avalon's friends spoke in a volume that would challenge a Richter scale, so Paige didn't feel that cut off. Avalon held her close and, dialogue or not, she was happy to be next to her.

They'd kissed when Avalon picked her up, and again at the stoplight on Santa Monica and Robertson. Paige wanted to kiss her again, and when she said something fairly inconsequential in Avalon's ear, Paige nipped her soft lobe. Avalon tilted her head back slightly and closed her eyes. An exhilarating thrill rushed through Paige and she was happy her loud moan wasn't audible.

❖

Avalon felt the softness of Paige's ear and an abrupt ache filled her. She needed to have her thighs wrapped around her again.

"I think it's time to leave," Avalon said, and whether Paige heard her or read her lips, she nodded earnestly.

They deposited their drinks on the bar top, and Avalon led her toward the front of the Abbey. As they passed back by the Cabana bar where the noise had dissipated, Avalon caught a flash of an arm reaching out to grab her.

It was Jessica.

She loathed the look in her ex's eyes. That familiar glare brimmed with derision and malice.

"I'm busy, Jessica," she said sharply, trying to match her stare.

"Who's your new friend?"

Avalon tried to get past Jessica's evil force field by jerking her arm out of the unpleasant grip. Jessica, however, planted her Victoria Beckham No Heel Boots expediently between Avalon and Paige.

Avalon gritted her teeth at the malevolent look Jessica aimed at Paige and cringed when she said, "What's your name, honey?"

"Jessica, really?" Avalon's temples started to pound.

"What?" she said, as an imitation of innocence dribbled from her lips.

"It's none of your business."

"As long as your dildos are still at my house, it is."

Now she was incensed. She moved Paige behind her to face off. "Don't start this."

"I'm not starting anything, baby. I'm just curious who's sharing your bed now."

"Leave it alone."

Jessica moved way too close. "Now, how am I supposed to leave it alone when we both know this little bitch, here, is just going to become collateral damage?"

"Shut the fuck up!" Her voice increased in volume with each word. "And get out of my face."

"There was a time, I recall fondly, when you didn't want me or my crotch out of your face."

Her peripheral vision caught a few cell phones pointed toward them, and though every muscle in her body tensed in cautious alarm, it was impossible to shutter her mouth.

"That's enough. It's over, Jessica. Get that through your fucking head."

Jessica's laughter erupted. "Oh, I'm not concerned about our breakup. I just don't want to see you run this poor girl over with your typical steamroller behavior."

"Keep her out of this, Jessica."

"I think it's too late, baby." She scanned the room like an overdramatic searchlight. "Your little date is already being uploaded by now."

Avalon leaned forward until her nose was almost touching Jessica's. "Fuck. You."

She wanted to show Paige that she was sorry, but her face was so tight with fury, she couldn't do anything but look at the ground and lead her out of the bar and straight to her car.

Paige hadn't uttered one word the whole time and Avalon couldn't blame her. She accelerated up Doheny and turned left on Santa Monica Boulevard. "I'm so sorry for that. I should have guessed Jessica would be out tonight."

She placed her hand on Paige's thigh, the silence between them made more agonizing as her hand lay there, untouched by Paige's. She stopped for a light and glanced her way. Paige stared straight ahead, as if she were watching zombies or some other surreal vision through the windshield.

"Paige? I'm really sorry about what she said."

"That doesn't bother me," Paige finally said. "But what you said does."

She hadn't expected that response. "She went on the attack. I was trying to defend you."

"That you had to talk to her at all is what I mean."

Avalon didn't understand. You couldn't just avoid engaging with the likes of Jessica. And she hadn't gotten where she had by backing down from about a million different situations. "People like that just don't go away quietly, Paige."

When she didn't get a response, she said, "Let's just go back to my place and—"

"Do you mind taking me home?"

"Paige," she said, "let's please not ruin tonight."

It wasn't until the light turned green that Paige finally said, "Then come over and we can unwind. Talk, maybe?"

That wasn't what she had pictured for the night exactly. She'd hoped they'd eventually end up in bed again, not just to have sex, but so she could understand more about what Avalon might be feeling for her.

Now, the discomfort of what had just happened with Jessica tainted the end of the evening, and while the sensible part of her thought it best to wind up the night right there, maybe some conversation could help. A little decompression would be better than ending on the sour, unpleasant note that currently tasted so disagreeable to her.

❖

Paige opened the leaded windows of her apartment, and the fresh aroma of night jasmine drifted in from the Villa Primavera courtyard. The fountain splished and splashed in its usual tête-à-tête, reminding her of a conversation between two old ladies.

"That's nice," Avalon said from the couch. She reached her hand out. "Come here."

"I'm really sorry about tonight," she said as Paige sat down.

"I'm not used to bar confrontations. They're so...public."

Avalon's chuckle seemed self-deprecating. "Yeah, they are."

"Don't get me wrong, I've had my share of fights, but I hate displays in front of other people. I just want a nice, normal evening out, you know?"

A furtive smirk emerged in spite of her efforts to suppress it. "Are you saying I'm not a nice, normal woman?"

"Not really. I mean, you're into your Hollywood world. Your life is like some extravagant meal of eggs Benedict with caviar and poached salmon. I'm like...eggs over easy."

"I happen to like eggs over easy."

"To be honest, I was halfway expecting some kind of outlandish moment tonight," Paige said. "I've got this thing about being in public. I'm not necessarily shy, but I hate to draw attention to myself."

"You do?"

She nodded. "I have to go out on a book tour in about five months and I'm petrified."

"Because you have to speak in front of people?"

"Yes."

"Well, as long as you don't go overboard like I do, you should be fine."

"No, really. I'm so scared. Like, I know I'm going to have a panic attack or pass out or something."

"That has to be frightening."

"It is."

"Sometimes I get nervous."

"No way."

"I do. It's a little different. I'm always afraid I'll trip or my tight dress will rip wide open."

"I'm sure you could cover with a witty quip or something."

Avalon laughed. "There'd still be a slew of photographs all over the Internet."

"Do you feel like you're susceptible to trouble every time you walk out the door?"

"It seems to follow actors around. If I had a nickel for every crazy thing I've seen or story I could tell—"

"Like what?"

"Drunken brawls, naked walks on Sunset Boulevard, crazy demands."

"What kind of demands?"

"I know someone who requires that," she said, making quotation marks in the air, "her path of travel must be prepared in advance with the scent of roses. Another one went on vacation, and when she came back and found her goldfish dead in the bowl, she fired all three assistants and her manager."

"Really?"

Avalon nodded. "A friend of mine has all the outside lights of her hotels turned off so she can see the stars. That's, of course, after she takes over a whole floor so she doesn't see anyone in the hall. And a very famous person, who I won't name, stabbed her agent with her high heels. Oh," she laughed, "and once, a costar insisted on having a big box of kitty litter in the corner of his dressing room."

"He had a cat?"

"No. He didn't want to walk to the bathroom."

"Are you kidding?"

"No. A celebrity can strip down to nothing, walk down Rodeo Drive, and rant about Popsicles and rainbows, but it's all explained away as their being dehydrated or overworked instead of just frickin' out of it because they went too far. How else do you explain an actor I know who wigged out at the Beverly Hilton, threw a chair out the window, showering glass all over everyone sitting around the pool below, then hung out the window and asked them to throw the chair back because he had nowhere to sit?"

Paige shook her head at the liberties celebrities were granted. Sure, it was part of the game of money and power, and many didn't handle either very well. It didn't help that their "handlers" were quick to acquiesce and then go about managing the damage control that ensued.

"I'm sorry that situation at the Abbey made you uncomfortable," Avalon said.

"I am, too." She was surprised she answered that way, but the confrontation really hadn't been okay, and she didn't want to tell Avalon it was.

Avalon looked a bit taken aback. "Listen, it was a fiery relationship and she makes me get so freakin' pissed off sometimes."

"What about just walking away?"

A partial laugh burbled out of her mouth. "When cameras are around? Paige, it's a different world for me. Everything is recorded these days, and I couldn't give them a shot of my tail between my legs." A small wave of regret seemed to settle in her expression. "Please accept my apology."

She softened and nodded. "Would you like anything? Wine? Water?"

"I'm fine, thank you." She picked up Paige's *The End* and started leafing through it. "How long have you been a photographer?"

"Since I was in my early twenties."

"What else have you done?"

"Before I started the Hollywood books, I published *The Landscape of a Woman*."

"That sounds intriguing. May I see it?"

She retrieved it from a small bookshelf, handing it to Avalon as she sat back down.

"Nude women," Avalon said as she turned each page, slowly studying the black-and-white images in the large-format book.

Quiet utterances of *wow* and *amazing* excited Paige. She was proud of that work and happily absorbed the compliments. "That used to be my bread and butter."

"Those are some nice loaves of bread."

She laughed. "That's about all I had to pay those models back then."

"These are beautiful." Avalon looked up and her green eyes seemed to sparkle with admiration.

"Thanks," she said as a flicker of desire tickled her.

Avalon kissed her and she tasted the leathery caramel of the French Connection cocktail she'd had earlier.

"Photograph me."

Paige nodded to the book. "Like that?"

"Yes."

"When?"

"Now."

"Now?"

Avalon laughed. "You've already seen me in the nude."

"I'm not sure I'd get much shot with you in the nude."

"Really?! Hmm, well, we'll try to stay professional."

She picked up her camera as Avalon stood and took her other hand. "Where do you want me?"

She was about to answer when Avalon pulled her toward the bedroom.

Only her two Moorish wall sconces were lit, casting long

shafts of golden light on the thickly textured stucco walls. She watched Avalon take in the room, with its rich, red area rug over the hardwood floor, the jacquard-draped windows, and the copper-and-ceramic ceiling fixture.

"Is there enough light in here?"

"Sure," she said, raw desire rising inside her.

Avalon began to undress and Paige froze in place. As if she had accidentally come upon Avalon removing her clothes by a quiet, undisturbed lake, she was transfixed by Avalon's beauty and the extreme sultriness of such a simple and everyday act.

When she had removed everything but her bra and panties, Avalon sat on the bed. She said nothing but gazed at her almost playfully. Paige's heart beat faster, trying to keep up with a symphony whose score was driving toward a rising crescendo of anticipation and craving.

She slowly brought the camera to her eye.

Avalon leaned back on her hands and Paige took some shots. Slowly, Avalon dropped her head back and Paige zoomed in on the line of her chin. She wanted to run her tongue across what she knew would be a hot, delicious curve.

She continued shooting as Avalon rolled over on her stomach. Paige moved to the side of the bed to catch the length of Avalon's body and watched as she pulled the pillow from under the quilt and clutched it.

Avalon looked as if she had just awoken from a sexy dream, one that still pervaded her mind and body, because she began to slowly drive her hips down against the bed as if trying to prolong the sensations.

Moving closer, Paige framed the viewfinder to document the gorgeous profile as Avalon's hair fell over her closed eyes.

Avalon turned onto her back, moving the pillow down over her breasts and stomach until it rested over her hips. Paige stopped tapping the shutter button as Avalon dipped her hands under the pillow. The sight made her suddenly light-headed, and she had to breathe faster to keep from passing out. She was wet immediately. When Avalon pulled off her panties, bringing them out from underneath the pillow, Paige lowered the camera.

Avalon slowly opened her eyes. "Keep shooting."

Obediently, she raised the camera, powerless to do anything but follow the commands.

Avalon sat up, straddling the pillow between her legs. Paige moaned loudly, receiving a wicked smile. The throbbing fullness between her legs made it harder to stand upright as Avalon's thighs hugged the pillow like it was the sole focus of her pleasure.

Avalon reached behind her and flicked off her bra. It slid down her side, falling to the bed by her knee. Paige zoomed in, framing the bra, the knee, and part of the pillow in an image she didn't need to record because it had been burned into her memory.

As she zoomed back out, Avalon was looking straight at her, rocking ever so attentively on the pillow.

The moment Avalon began to open her mouth, Paige captured only one frame before Avalon said, "I want you."

Paige dropped the camera.

"Come here."

She found Avalon's mouth immediately, kissing her hard and pushing her down on the bed. Avalon bit her bottom lip and Paige's hips involuntarily tightened, thrusting into her thigh, but the pillow was in the way. She reached down, pulling the barrier from between them, and chucked it to the side of the bed.

Avalon moaned loudly, raking at Paige's clothes, almost tearing them off. Paige helped her, not caring if everything ended up shredded. She needed her now and reached between her thighs.

"You're so wet," she said as she felt the extraordinary silkiness between her fingers. Gently, she slid two fingers inside. Avalon moaned—intense, amazing noises—as Paige buried her head in her neck, sucking warm skin that tasted of heady vanilla.

Paige moved her hips in rhythm with her fingers and heard Avalon say, "Yesssss."

Breathing heavily, Avalon rolled them so they were now on their sides, Paige still stroking her. And when Paige felt Avalon's fingers traveling up her thigh and down across her hip, she shifted to give her more room. She had to feel her, to be filled by her. Even though she knew what would happen, the moment Avalon plunged inside her, she called out suddenly, surrendering to the sweet primal need that rushed inside her.

She found Avalon's mouth, kissing her greedily as Avalon pushed deeper.

Avalon broke the kiss, saying, "Fuck me," and Paige's brain raced into overdrive. The sublime dizziness from her shameless need felt like a narcotic.

"Yes," Avalon coaxed her, "harder."

The heat between them broke into a light, moist haze of exertion. Paige wanted to melt into her, to get lost in a communal, hot passion that would absolutely devour them.

Their rhythm was magnificently matched, stroke for stroke, and when Avalon slowed, so did Paige. The way they fit together, the way they responded to each other felt so right—just like it had from the first moment they'd touched.

Avalon's fingers seemed to be taking her over. She moved inside her with such passion it was practically spiritual.

A sudden tug of vulnerability gripped her. Paige recognized the change in her feelings. She knew she wanted Avalon but in a way that far exceeded the lust of the moment. Desire tumbled inside out, and she let go of any questions or reservations about who she was with.

She closed her eyes, wanting her, needing her, in a deeper, more serious way now.

She held Avalon tighter, savoring her as long as possible. Avalon seemed to understand because her moan purred out like a hallowed acquiescence.

Paige opened her eyes and found Avalon's concentrated gaze penetrating her. Nose to nose, they moved in the perfect measure of a steady but building musical composition, taking the time for each exquisite note. No clocks existed—no phones, no outside world. Everything that wasn't part of their flesh and bone melted away, leaving only the arousing sounds of their lovemaking and the sweet agony of their desire.

Paige kept a steady, sensual cadence, feeling Avalon's body react and counter. She listened to her breathing, convinced that her own existence was dependent upon it.

And then Avalon whispered, "Come for me."

Paige's hips responded, pushing into Avalon, who met her with deep plunges of her fingers.

Paige reached deeper as well. Avalon gasped, then exhaled loudly. "Yes!"

"I want you to come harder than you ever have," Paige told her through her own struggle for breath.

And with powerful pushes, as if they were on a surfboard racing for the next wave's crest, they moved in unison, panting in erotic exertion until they reached the highest peak and crashed into the enormous tidal wave of their orgasms.

Chapter Thirteen

The director yelled "cut" and Avalon walked back to her director's chair, sitting down with extreme relief. She could finally take a break from using her brain. Paige had been on her mind so much that entire day she was surprised she hadn't used her name when referring to her costar.

She had fallen so hard for Paige. Never had she let someone so deep inside her. Sure, they'd only been together twice, but the intensity that surged through her when she felt Paige's touch was still palpable.

She raised her fingers to her lips, recalling how Paige's mouth felt on hers. And when she replayed the rush that came when Paige slipped her fingers inside her, she bent forward in her chair, groaning quietly.

Paige was perfection. Her heart was kind and genuine, and her body was as hot as she could ever long for. Though Paige was certainly reserved and predictable, all that fell away when they were intimate.

It surprised her that there hadn't been any of the typical strings or warning signs that had accompanied the start of her previous relationships. She'd always sensed forewarnings of scandal or trouble, signs she would ignore with defiance, only to find her life turned upside down with a nasty breakup and her life empty of everything but a handful of regret.

Overlooking Jessica's abrasive personality had been a

mistake. She hadn't learned the same lesson with previous lovers either, believing she could have whatever she wanted, regardless of who thought or said what. And it seemed everyone had something to say.

How much of her troubles had the press caused? Had her previous chances at love been sabotaged from the beginning? Gossip could undermine the strongest of unions, chipping away at the foundation, weakening confidence and trust.

Then again, even when the press wasn't around, she and Jessica were like a torch to dry kindle, igniting arguments without much provocation.

And all of that was absent with Paige.

"Lighting will be done in ten minutes," Helen said as she approached. "Do you want Tawnya to touch up your makeup and hair?"

She nodded, knowing she'd have to somehow manage the rest of her scenes with the essence of Paige wrapped tightly around her.

❖

Ricky Boswell avoided performing any of his own stunts, a practice that wasn't unique in a town where legs, arms, and faces were insured for millions of dollars, but one he pursued to the extreme.

Stunt people were always brought in to execute complicated and dangerous action scenes, but an actor's ego usually compelled him to get as much camera time as possible. Because of that, minor stunts were choreographed to allow face recognition. This made the audience believe that the star had carried out all of the daring feats.

But while sports cars were careening about or punches were being thrown, Ricky was usually comfortably ensconced in his motor home, feet kicked up on the coffee table, martini in hand.

And that's exactly where Paige was at that moment, tape recorder in hand, wondering how the hell she was going to work this lazy bit of truth into her book.

"It's a well-known fact," Ricky was saying, "that without the face of the film, there is no film. You see, people want to connect with a star, not just the story. They want to *be* that star. So, in essence, I am their warrior."

"Warrior?"

Ricky pursed his lips as if placating a small child who asked where hamburgers come from. "Yes. People's lives are drab. They go to the movies to escape. And I am there to take them on a journey of bravery and fortitude, of wisdom and triumph."

"This movie is called *Chocolate Milk and Cake*."

"Chocolate is a metaphor. It represents lust and greed. The warrior needs to protect civilization from that."

Paige couldn't even bring herself to raise her camera to capture such drivel. She had already gotten quite a few tremendous shots of Paul, Ricky's stunt double, in action. He was an extremely pleasant and energetic man who attacked all the hazardous stunts with enthusiasm and a whoop of exhilaration each time the director yelled "cut."

And as she sat with Ricky, trying to pull out anything of interest that didn't revolve around his extreme self-love, she decided that Paul would find a place in her book as well. He wasn't a star, but he was dynamic enough to write about. She'd add a section about the people who stood in the shadows, people whose bodies were seen in motion but whose faces were always obscured.

Her spirits brightened for the first time since she'd stepped into the slimy puddle of Ricky's ego sludge. She allowed him to continue his diatribe, even taking a few shots to document his repugnant lethargy, and let her thoughts wander to Avalon.

The night before had been a little rushed, but what else could she have done after the way Avalon had posed for her? The pull of her natural sexuality had been too attractive to resist, but so was Avalon as a person.

In many ways, Avalon was the opposite of her—brash where she was modest, outspoken where she was diplomatic, fearless where she was timorous. And she flew by the seat of her pants whereas Paige kept more grounded. In a world where Avalon stirred things up, Paige couldn't even find the spoon.

And all that contradiction worked like a magnet close to iron, enticing her and drawing her toward Avalon so powerfully that Paige couldn't drive her desire away if she'd tried.

People talked about the stars aligning, but Paige knew it was much more than that. The way she felt about Avalon was tantamount to a stratospheric explosion.

❖

"The Chateau Marmont is booked for next Friday, darling," Carmen said when she called Paige that afternoon.

Paige's hands-free phone allowed her to maneuver through the traffic in Hollywood as she headed to Chris's house for dinner. Sunset Boulevard was packed with commuters, but the side streets would be too, so she stayed where she was.

"Okay. I'll tell Avalon. Thanks for arranging it."

"It's gratis, so make sure you credit them in the texts or photos."

"No problem."

"You've got less than two months, you know."

"Don't remind me."

"Do you have an idea for the cover yet?"

"I'm hoping that one from the Marmont will be it."

"Even though it won't be an action shot?"

"I'm bringing a lot of stunt gear. I'm picturing her by the pool, on a chaise lounge, dressed to the nines, but with all this grungy gear around her."

"That's a great idea."

As Sunset Boulevard curved slightly at North Kings Road, a billboard came into view. Avalon Randolph was displayed front and center, sitting on the letters of the name of her recent film. Those incredible lips had to be two feet wide. But it was her hand that made Paige almost brake in the middle of traffic. Not twelve hours ago, those fingers had been inside her, pleasuring her and driving her wild.

"Oh, my God—"

"What?"

"Nothing. I'll…I'll have something to show you next week."

Chris's house sat on Palm Avenue, between Sunset and Santa Monica Boulevard. It was a small bungalow squished between rather bland, mid-century modern apartment buildings of pale stucco and nondescript balconies. Her diminutive dwelling was unassuming, but cheerful with its light blue paint and chocolate trim.

Abel barked from the backyard as Paige knocked on the door and then stepped in.

"Officer Bergstrom, show yourself."

"I'm marinating," she called from the kitchen.

"I doubt you'd ever get tenderized enough to be tasty," Paige said as she entered the kitchen and poked her in the ribs.

"That's what you think." Chris uncovered the foil from a dish that held two steaks. "You're just in time. Follow me."

Abel barked again, trotting up to smell the back of Paige's hand. Chris put the steaks on her barbeque and pointed to the patio table nearby. "Beer okay?"

Paige opened both bottles and handed one to her. "Perfect."

"I made potato salad, I hope that's all right."

"You're such a housewife."

"You obviously haven't seen the laundry room."

"As stinky as you and Abel get? I won't anytime soon. How are things in the life of my K9 copper?"

"Great. He got his third bite last night."

"Really?"

"Yeah. Some knucklehead wouldn't come out of a house we were serving with a warrant. I called four times, told him I'd release my dog, and the idiot stayed put."

"I bet he regrets that now."

"Yeah, all twenty-eight stitches of that decision."

"Ouch."

"But it was a good night. We seized ten grams of meth and five thousand dollars."

"Nice."

"How was your second date?"

"Good. Great. Weird."

"In that order?"

"No, the weird started first. We were at the Abbey and Jessica showed up."

"Jessica, as in Jessica Wiley?"

"Yup."

"Did it get ugly?" Chris turned the steaks over and then pulled her cell phone from the pocket of her shorts.

"You could say that. Avalon flew off the handle and caused a scene. I mean, Jessica was in her face, but it was all too dramatic for me."

"Yikes," Chris said as she tapped on her phone.

"We talked about it after. I told her I'm just not used to drama and craziness."

"That, you're not."

"It certainly wasn't fun."

"It doesn't look like you were having fun." Chris turned her cell phone so that Paige could see the screen. The video was shaky and a little dark, but it captured the whole confrontation.

"Shit."

"There are more angles of it. Wanna see?"

"No. That's enough." Paige put her beer down. "Damn it."

"It's to be expected. Come on, you're dating a celebrity."

"Not all celebrities act like that."

"How is she in private?"

"Not that way at all. She's kind and sexy and funny, actually."

"So she's got a public personality. I doubt it's who she really is."

"It's part of who she is."

"What? You don't have bad parts? Come on, I've seen you when you haven't gotten enough sleep."

Paige glared at her.

"How was the rest of the night?"

Wonderful couldn't describe it fully. "Fantastic, tremendous, remarkable."

"Wow, all those?"

"I'm crazy about her."

"That's awesome!"

"It's going so fast."

Chris sat down next to her. "This isn't the era of Victorian prudishness. It's perfectly all right to race down the road of romance."

"I'm not a prude. I'm just nervous. What if she dumps me without even a phone call? What if she stomps on my heart?"

"Your heart has been stomped on before and you survived."

"Easy for you to say."

"No, it's not easy for me to say. Jen nearly killed me when she left. Would I have been with her if I knew she'd eventually leave? Yes. I loved her. So I took the chance."

She was right. Still, Avalon seemed like a race car with no brakes. And Paige's heart was now strapped to the hood.

But what could she do? She wanted her.

❖

Early Wednesday morning, Paige was making notes for the Chateau Marmont shoot. She had two days to rent equipment and arrange the props that would enhance her chosen theme. Most of the phone calls were made and as she waited for some answers back, she grabbed a pad of paper and began sketching ideas of some photo compositions.

Her doorbell rang. Chris was at work, so it wasn't her, and other than some wonderfully sexy texts she'd shared with Avalon, they hadn't spoken since their last night together.

A tall man in a well-tailored black suit stood at the door.

"Are you Paige Cornish?"

"Yes?"

"Avalon Randolph would like to meet with you. I'm here to pick you up. She wanted me to ask if you were free for about twelve hours."

"Twelve hours?"

"Maybe more. She would also like you to pack a jacket and wear hard-soled shoes."

His demeanor gave away no more information, and judging by the serious look on his face, she doubted she'd get more by asking specific questions.

The Marmont shoot was coming together and she could answer her cell phone from anywhere, so she actually did have twelve hours, or more, free.

Curiosity tiptoed up her spine. What was Avalon planning?

❖

The driver took her to the Bob Hope Airport in Burbank. Rather than arriving at the departure terminal, he drove to the private-jet section and out onto the tarmac. Passing a few planes that were tied to the ground, they headed for one that was pointing toward the runway.

"What's this?" Paige said under her breath. Obviously, she'd spoken loud enough for the driver to respond, "This is a Learjet 60."

That wasn't really what she was asking, but as soon as he came to a stop next to the plane's staircase, Avalon stepped out and walked down to greet her. Paige's mouth was open as she got out of the limo, and she was about to repeat her question when Avalon took her in her arms and squeezed her.

"Now don't protest," Avalon said quickly, then kissed her.

"Why would I protest?" Was this going to be a flight to San Francisco for lunch? Maybe a trip to Catalina Island for some sightseeing?

"We're going to Oklahoma!"

Paige shook her head as if she hadn't heard her correctly. "Oklahoma?"

The pilot appeared at the top of the steps. Avalon took her hand and they ascended the stairs. Behind the pilot stood a flight attendant and the copilot. They all greeted her by name and stepped aside.

Paige had never been in a private jet before. It had only seven seats, which looked more like big, white leather massage chairs. The interior walls were impeccably white and the thick carpet was silver-gray. A rather large fold-down table in front of the first two seats held a platter of fresh-cut vegetables, fruit, and breads. Little beads of moisture on a champagne bottle glistened from the sun as it rested in a silver bucket. Next to that were, Paige assumed from the sparkle, two cut-crystal flutes.

"Buckle up," Avalon said as she sat down.

Paige lowered herself into the seat, buckled her belt, and turned to Avalon. "Oklahoma?"

"Curious, aren't you?"

"Very."

Avalon took her hand. "You'll see soon enough."

The pilot slowly eased the jet down the runway, and as they gained speed, Paige watched the city of Burbank move by her window and then slowly fall away as the jet climbed rather swiftly toward the clouds.

When they'd leveled out, the flight attendant stepped up and asked if they wanted champagne. Paige, still quite surprised, just looked to Avalon.

"Yes, please."

As quickly as the attendant appeared, she was gone. Paige wondered if that's what the private part of private jet meant.

"To an adventure," Avalon said as she held up her glass.

"An adventure?"

The look on Avalon's face seemed to be a mix of excitement and delight, and her eyes had never looked so bright. "I know the only things you've uttered so far are questions, but I assure you, the answers are forthcoming." She shifted closer. "And for now, let's just enjoy the time without cell phones and other distractions." They kissed and Paige felt that wonderfully soft tongue that had pleased her so well the last time they'd been together.

Avalon began to tenderly caress her face, and Paige relaxed into the sensation, enjoying the reassurance of Avalon's affection.

She decided that wherever they were going didn't matter. Being together did.

❖

Three hours later, the jet touched down in Oklahoma City. Paige had no idea what the name of the airport was as they taxied to a small building whose sign read *Executive Charter*. Though it was only one o'clock in the afternoon, the cloudy skies were battleship gray. A few droplets of rain tapped against the windows, as if wanting to get her attention.

They deplaned and the pilot confirmed that Avalon had his cell-phone number to contact him for their return. She didn't give him a time, which intrigued Paige.

A large, black SUV was parked close by and someone who looked like the Marlboro man stepped out. He wore a wide-brimmed cowboy hat, jeans, and a checkered shirt under his brown vest. His scruffy boots looked like they'd seen more than a few cattle drives.

Avalon walked Paige over to him.

"Paige, this is Rusty McNamara. Rusty, this is Paige Cornish."

He tipped his hat, saying, "Ma'am." Turning to Avalon, he said, "We'd better get going. I've got a good feeling about today."

He opened the SUV's back door for them to climb in. As they did, Paige's curiosity spiked even higher when she saw that the front seat and dashboard were filled with strange-looking equipment that blinked and hummed and hissed of static.

"Okay," she finally said. "What's going on?"

Rusty climbed in the car and started the engine.

"You and I," Avalon said, hardly containing her excitement, "are going storm chasing!"

"What?"

"We're in tornado alley and Rusty is an expert chaser. He's also a meteorologist. We're on the hunt for supercells!"

"Are you serious?"

"You said you'd like to do this one day, and today's the day."

"Are you serious?"

Avalon nodded enthusiastically.

"I can't believe it!"

Christmas had arrived early and she had the best present of all. As she hugged Avalon, Rusty drove out of the airport and they were on their way.

"We're heading to Elk City, Oklahoma," Rusty said when they were on the interstate. "The largest tornado there was in 1955. A category F4 blew through, killing two people and injuring eighteen, I believe."

"Will we see a tornado?" Paige asked.

"It's not a guarantee, but hopefully we'll find a supercell."

Paige felt giddy with anticipation. "How does this work?"

"It's all about forecasting and trying to understand the inner workings of weather," Rusty said as he stared at the road ahead of him. Rain began to fall harder and he turned on his windshield wipers. "We study severe weather outlooks, computer model forecasts, and things like that. All this equipment around me here helps with that." He pointed to things without looking down. "This is my anemometer to measure wind speed, there's the thermometer, and that hygristor is for taking humidity readings."

Paige said, "What do you look for?"

"A storm worth chasing will have the right combination of moisture, instability, lift, and wind shear. For the storm that's forming in Elk City, I've been analyzing surface and upper-air data for the last three days. I look to see where the four factors are setting up and where they may shift. As of this morning, I've been able to narrow down the data and that's where we're heading. I'll keep watch over the weather maps and satellite pictures on my laptop, but when we get there, the real data ends up in the sky itself. She'll tell us where to go."

"And what exactly is a supercell?"

"It's the presence of a mesocyclone, which is a deep, persistently rotating updraft. It's a special class of thunderstorms that tend to produce the most and strongest tornadoes. We're looking for vertical wind shear, which is a change in wind direction and speed with height."

Avalon snuggled close to Paige. "You are so attractive when you're curious."

As they watched lightning flicker on the western horizon, Paige pointed to it. "I imagine running into a tornado is the most dangerous part of storm chasing."

"Not really. Running into chase crowds is. Those are made up of inexperienced yee-haws who are unpleasant and very hazardous. They drive crazy, park in the middle of the road, and cause a lot of accidents. Lightning is also dangerous, and so is hail. A softball-size chunk of ice can cause some major damage."

"Do you expect any of those things today?" Avalon said.

"I know how to avoid the chase crowds, but I can't vouch for Mother Nature."

A walkie-talkie came to life as a static-filled voice called out some numbers. Rusty picked up the radio and began talking to someone called Bud.

Paige turned to Avalon. "I can't thank you enough for this. I'm astonished that you did it for me."

"I'm glad you were open to an adventure."

"This is more than that. You remembered my crazy dream of storm chasing."

"I remember all of our talks."

Paige kissed her, and the sweetness of their touch was more perfect than anything she could imagine. "Aren't your...people wondering where you are?"

"I told Michele D. and Billy I was going rogue today. I assured them I wouldn't be around any paparazzi, so they calmed down."

Rusty signed off the radio. "Well, ladies, a couple of friends of mine are just to the west of us, and they tell me we're heading in the right direction. If we're lucky, there could be a convective development within a couple of hours."

"What's that?"

"It's the rising or sinking of air. You see, hot air weighs less than cold air, so when both hot and cold air are in the same place, the cold air sinks and the hot air rises. That's what makes a hot-air balloon float. As hot air rises, it pushes the cold air out of the way. Then it hits more cold air and pushes that down and keeps rising. That's what's called a thermal."

Avalon said, "It sounds like a lot of waiting around."

Rusty laughed. "It is. But there's still a lot to see. The skies are always magnificent when they're active. Keep looking west." He pointed in the direction they were heading. "When lightning streaks overhead and casts a silver glow across the landscape, that's called an anvil crawler."

For the next twenty minutes, they watched in silence. The sky resembled a huge Morse code machine with dots and dashes of lightning punctuating the oncoming darkness. The message was clear that an approaching storm was building. They were starting to get closer and could hear the low rumble of thunder.

A half hour later, the storm was much nearer and Rusty pointed toward the northwest. "Do you see those clouds that have globes hanging down from them? That's called a cumulonimbus mammatus. They're a good sign because they can indicate a particularly strong storm, even a tornadic storm."

"So we might see a tornado after all?"

"Possibly."

"And look. Up ahead."

A large white truck, carrying a flatbed that housed a radar, had just turned onto the interstate.

"That's a DOW, a Doppler on Wheels. They map tornado winds and can analyze tornado structure."

"So we're on the right track?" Paige said.

"I'd say we definitely are."

They passed the Elk City sign and Paige's excitement grew. She scanned the flat landscape dotted with scrub trees bowing to what must have been fairly strong winds. The rain continued to fall, pelting the top of the SUV in a staccato rhythm that seemed to be tapping out the details of an unfolding electrifying prophecy.

Avalon gripped her arm and they snuggled as close as their seat belts would allow.

Rusty caught up with the Doppler on Wheels and radioed them.

"DOW7447, this is KA4ERO listening on 24.119 Elk City. Copy?"

"DOW7447. Rusty, is that you?"

"I'm right behind you, Phil."

"Great day for a performance from the heavens."

"It sure is."

"We're turning off at North 1980 and heading toward Beaver Dam Creek."

"Great minds think alike. We've got your back."

"Great. We could use your noggin."

"It's free to you, Phil."

Rusty signed off. "Their presence in this vicinity is a good thing. We're going to join forces on this one."

As they left the interstate, the road became less and less taken care of. She couldn't see any signs, just a long stretch of barbed wire fences on either side of them. The ride became rough and bouncy as the hard-packed gravel kicked up dust around them. Soon, potholes punctuated the asphalt like Morse code spelling out the words *here we go!*

A whirl of excitement coursed through Paige. She thought of her first roller-coaster ride when she was eleven years old. She was with her best friend and they were heading for a corn-dog stand when her friend diverted them to the coaster queue. She'd never considered going on such a monstrous attraction, but with the voices of all her friends ramping up in excitement, she went along with it without thinking about how tall the steel tracks soared above her. It wasn't until she got in the coaster car and began to ascend that she regretted her spur-of-the-moment decision. She'd never been so scared, thoroughly believing that every drop would be her last and that every turn would be the one that caused the car to jump the tracks, plummeting her to her death. She screamed so loudly that she spent the rest of the day drinking sodas to soothe her sore, raw throat. And while that coaster ride had been her last, she was proud she'd survived it.

Here she was again, following someone to the coaster queue. And she felt proud again. She leaned over and kissed Avalon. "I guess this trip is forcing me to be a little more impulsive."

"I hope. When we first talked about your fantasy of storm chasing, you said that being impulsive doesn't come easily to you. I knew if I asked you beforehand, you might think too much about the consequences and not go. So I hope you'll be glad you did."

"As long as we don't end up flying through the air like Dorothy from Kansas, I'll be fine."

Avalon looked at her with the same bedroom eyes she'd seen when she photographed her in her room. "Don't look at me that way or I'll have to tell Rusty to drop us off at an Elk City motel, and pronto."

"I just love the way spontaneous looks on you."

"Does it go with my eyes?"

Avalon kissed her. "Yes. And your lips and your ears, and your..." She strained to bury her head in Paige's neck but the seat belt made her grunt. "Damn. Backseats aren't as much fun as they used to be."

"Well, if there's a tornado, everyone will be focused on that, so we can stay right here and take care of things."

Avalon raised her eyebrows dramatically. "You wouldn't miss the opportunity to see a tornado, would you?"

"Hmm," Paige said, scrunching her lips together in deliberation. "Difficult decision."

The truck shook forcefully and Paige jumped. Outside her window, branches and large chunks of green and brown material buffeted the SUV. The rain had let up a bit, but the ferocity of the elements surprised her.

"This is a good place," Rusty said, and radioed Phil. They concurred, and both vehicles pulled over to the side of the road.

"Be careful when you get out. Watch for flying objects and listen to me. If I tell you to get back into the car, don't wait to take a few more pictures. Get back in, okay?"

Paige and Avalon nodded.

The wind made it difficult to open the door, but Paige finally pushed it hard and she and Avalon stepped out onto the shoulder. Phil and a couple of other men darted over to them and started talking to Rusty.

The countryside was alive with commotion. Trees swayed in unison and a highway sign shimmied like a drug addict in withdrawal. Squinting against the pelting rain, Paige listened to the sharp whir of wind as it buffeted her ears and foretold the approach of things much more mighty.

Rusty came over to them and pointed up. "That big dark cloud about two or three miles away, right there, is called a cumulonimbus. See the black flat base and extremely high top? The warm air that has risen has met warmer air and can't go any higher, so the bottom spreads out. The anvil shape is a good sign that we'll see some spectacular things."

"The cloud itself is amazing."

"She's a beauty, all right. Updrafts are happening inside, and the rain that's falling is creating a downdraft. The simultaneous presence of both tells us we're in the mature stage of the storm." He stopped and stared at the cloud. "Man, the internal turbulence is ripe! Look at the movement!"

The cloud roiled like a magnificent beast reacting to someone stirring it from slumber. Its brute force both mesmerized and frightened Paige.

The wind picked up again and the gusts forced them to sway forward for balance.

They watched it for about forty-five minutes, and Paige and Avalon took pictures on their cell phones. The Doppler guys were in and out of their truck, probably recording information and watching for developments.

"Earlier," Rusty said, "I talked about using visual clues from the sky. The radar and weather information can get us to a general vicinity, but then we have to actually look for visual clues and," he said as he pointed again, "that one's starting to rotate."

Just then, Phil yelled, "We got rotation!"

Rusty started back toward the car. "Stay right here."

When he returned, he said, "I'm picking up wind speeds of up to sixty miles an hour. Since visibility is pretty good, I'm going to move us back a bit." He hollered to Phil and made a jerking motion with his arm. Phil obviously understood because he waved.

Rusty drove them backward a ways and they got back out of the SUV. As they did, the sound of a popcorn machine made Paige and Avalon look around.

"That's hail," he said. "Not too big, but it's another good sign."

Paige was awestruck. Nothing she'd ever seen on television or the Internet could sufficiently portray what she was feeling. Mother Nature was flexing her muscles and reminding the world that she was in control.

The cloud slowly revolved, seeming to grow larger, and then Paige saw a forelock-type of wisp descend from the bottom.

"Rusty, what's that?"

"The spinning is pulling the cloud down. That's the start of a tornado."

"Holy cow!" Avalon yelled. "That's freakin' awesome!"

"Here we go," Rusty said. "Don't forget to take pictures."

In fact, Paige had been so captivated by the show, her cell phone sat forsaken in her dangling hand. She clicked some images and then flipped it to video mode. The wisp grew larger, as if it was reaching down toward something to connect with. Hail clopped down around her and a few chunks jabbed her head and hands, but the sight was so hypnotizing, she didn't care.

It wasn't until Rusty, raising his voice over the increasing wind, said to them, "Get back in the car," that she stopped filming.

When they closed the doors, she realized she was out of breath—not from exertion but from the struggle to breathe in the wind and probably from the adrenaline that had rapidly peaked inside her.

"Watch," Rusty said as a longer funnel slowly formed, hovering over the fields.

"It doesn't look like it's moving now," Avalon said.

"It's definitely moving. That funnel is descending, which means the rotation speed is increasing. It'll be an official tornado when it touches the ground. At that point, its speed and power will escalate because it'll feed on the warmer surface air closer to the ground then."

Rusty started the SUV and Paige knew that meant he was getting ready to retreat if the tornado decided to head toward them. Her heart pounded and the exhilaration made her feel a little tipsy.

Slowly the thin funnel began to elongate and creep toward the ground as if it were a hungry but stealthy snake approaching an unsuspecting mouse. When it finally touched ground, a silent explosion erupted, sending debris in all directions. The ensuing cloud billowed out and Paige scrambled to turn her cell's video back on.

"That's so incredible…" Avalon's voice trailed off and Paige felt a hand squeezing her shoulder.

The swirling shaft undulated in the middle, as if using its momentum to gorge on more land. It twisted along the ground, gobbling up trees and fields of whatever crop was in its path. Debris flew out of the base in all directions.

"How big is that tornado?" Paige asked.

"It's probably a category F0 or F1. I'd guess the wind speed is between sixty and a hundred miles per hour. It's not a big one, but it can peel off roofs, knock down a detached garage, or push a car off the road. I'm glad there aren't any structures out here because I wouldn't want to have that twister prove it to you."

"It's astounding."

They watched it for a few minutes and suddenly the funnel withdrew, rising like the agile hand of a pianist from the keys of a just-completed concerto, then vanished in a swirling poof that dissipated into nothing. The rain's power fizzled away as well, and they watched for a few more minutes as the cloud appeared to relax and release its anger.

Suddenly, the quiet in the car was palpable. Like

experiencing the pause after the last smashing cymbals of an orchestral symphony, they sat still, stunned at the environmental performance they'd just witnessed. It felt like a sacred moment, hallowed and spiritual.

Rusty's radio hissed and Phil said, "Beautiful." He picked up the mouthpiece and they began to communicate using some scientific jargon.

"You did it!" Avalon suddenly said. "You're a storm chaser!"

"Wow." Paige shook her head. "We just saw a real tornado."

Avalon grabbed her, engulfing her in a strong hug. "My little tempting temptress of tempests!" They stared at each other for a moment and simultaneously howled their excitement in whoops and cheers so loud Rusty began to laugh.

CHAPTER FOURTEEN

Just outside the bungalow at the Chateau Marmont, Paige had spent the last hour shooting pictures of Avalon. They were exactly as she'd envisioned them. Avalon wore a bright yellow bikini, which brought out the blond in her hair. She lay on a dark blue chaise lounge with stunt harnesses, elbow and knee guards, a rope and pulley, and something called a Bohn Buttsaver draped around her. On the ground next to the lounge, a menacing-looking air ram sat next to a delicate blue martini.

The juxtaposition of dainty and rough elements was perfect for the cover shot of *Cut to the Chase*.

Lush and dense green foliage surrounded the pool area, masking whatever lay beyond. The muted, dark red brick hardscape created an ideal frame around the crisp, blue water. Six or seven people were lying out around the pool, and while they seemed more than interested in the photo shoot, they stayed to themselves. Tawnya and a wardrobe person were waiting inside the bungalow to freshen Avalon up, but so far, the overcast day had been ideal for staving off sweat and the need for a costume change.

"Come here," Avalon said when Paige moved around to her other side to get more shots.

Having watched Avalon slug down a few drinks during the shoot made Paige slightly uncomfortable. Things usually went poorly when alcohol tagged along on their dates. The photo shoot was going well, but Avalon could alter a situation as quickly and unpredictably as a natural gas explosion could level a building. Paige just needed to finish the shoot, get what she needed, and then she and Avalon could go to her house, maybe, and relax.

"Not yet," Paige said as she stepped a little further away. "I know what happened last time you said that, and I need to finish."

"I'll finish you."

"I'm convinced of that, but just a few more…" Through her viewfinder, she saw Avalon's expression change. Her smile fell away and she froze. Paige followed her line of sight. Jessica approached, with five other women trailing her. Paige recognized a couple of them from that night at the Abbey.

"Don't mind us," Jessica said as they passed them and deposited themselves in lounge chairs about twenty feet away.

Paige couldn't read Avalon's mood. Her gut knotted with nervous anticipation and she clutched her camera.

"Are we done?" Avalon said.

"Sure."

She put her camera down and had begun to pick up the stunt equipment when Avalon quickly pulled her down onto the lounge. She landed hard, half-straddling Avalon.

"What are you doing?"

Avalon reached up to the back of Paige's neck and drew her in for a kiss. She wrenched back but Avalon pulled even harder. The aggression shocked her. Paige felt Avalon's other hand snake its way around her ass, dipping forcefully under her pants.

"Avalon," she struggled to say, but Avalon held on tight. "Don't do this."

Avalon grabbed Paige's hair.

"Avalon—"

"Fuck her."

Paige pushed off Avalon and awkwardly got on her feet. "What did you say?"

"Fuck her. She needs to know I'm no longer available and to quit harassing me."

A raucous eruption of laughter came from Jessica and her friends. Through the catcalls, Paige heard them say, "Look! A lovers' quarrel!" and "Just enjoy the rough play, baby." Their vicious amusement sickened her as much as Avalon's grip on her neck.

Avalon seized Paige's hand, saying, "Don't make a scene, goddamnit."

A cyclone of anger and embarrassment swirled around Paige, suddenly heating her cheeks and threatening to make her cry. With a violent lurch, she dislodged Avalon's wrist. Avalon tried to snatch her again and Paige yanked her hand away. She thought she might choke on a gasp that lurched from her stomach. "Don't you ever do something like that to me again."

"What? Paige, come on. Don't be a baby. It's a fuck-you thing."

She heard noise to her right and looked up to see Tawnya and the wardrobe person watching from the bungalow door. From the other side, Jessica said, "Are you getting this on your cell?"

Her arms and legs went numb and her ears began to ring. A lone sob seized in her throat and then suddenly escaped as a discomfited yelp. She grabbed her camera and ran out of the pool area and straight to her car.

❖

"Are you home?"

"No."

"Okay, no-one-there, answer the door."

Paige sighed, fruitlessly straightening her crumpled T-shirt, and opened the door.

"You look like hell."

"Thanks for the encouragement." She walked away, leaving Chris to close the door and follow her to the kitchen.

"How long does one suffer from a breakup after a few dates?"

Paige frowned at her. "Are you trying to depress me even more?"

"No. I just think you should look at this in context. You haven't been out of your place for two weeks."

She opened a box of Cheerios and reached in. "I'm working."

"You're avoiding."

She stared at the handful of cereal. Tiny little carbohydrate lifesavers, useless for any rescue attempt. She stuffed them in her mouth. "Ah, Chris, I—"

"Chew," Chris said, folding her arms across her chest.

She swallowed. "I liked her so much. I think I was falling for her. I know I was."

"And she hurt you."

"I was so embarrassed. The scene at the Abbey, and then the crap at the Chateau. It was awful, Chris."

"So, what's the plan?"

She offered the box to Chris. "Cheerios and tears."

Chris shook her head. "That has been the plan. We need a new one."

She put the box down. "Get dressed?"

"I'd also shower first."

She shrugged. "That's all I've got."

Chris pulled a folded-up paper from her pocket. "Dee Jae wanted me to get this to you. It's a workshop she's doing. It starts tonight."

She unfolded the paper. Dee Jae was teaching playwriting at her theater.

"You focus on your book and then go to the workshops at night. That'll keep your mind off things. Plus, you know I'll be by a lot."

"I need to change my phone number."

"Has Avalon been calling?"

Paige nodded.

"And?"

"She's apologized in her voice mails and says she wants me back."

"Okay. So, what do you need?"

"I don't need the drama. I don't need the façade of celebrity rammed up my ass."

"Wow."

"I'm pissed."

"I thought you were falling for her."

"I was."

"Doesn't that mean she had some good points?"

"Yes. She did." Avalon's arms came to mind, how they'd wrapped so affectionately around her that first night. She really *liked* her. Their time alone together was so beautiful in so many ways, from the conversations to the lovemaking. And the trip to Oklahoma had been such a pleasant surprise and so endearing. But the black and white of Avalon's public behavior ping-ponged in her brain. "I felt like a pawn in her nasty little game."

"Do you really believe that?"

Paige stared at the Cheerios box, wishing the little rings were much bigger so she could keep from drowning in confusion. "I don't know."

"Well, you don't need to know right now. But Dee Jae's expecting you tonight."

Where else did she have to go? She'd stared at her walls long enough and couldn't rid her mind of Avalon. Nothing she had tried could jettison the memories of her from her mind, and she felt nothing but hopelessness. Like an alcoholic struggling to find solace from her demon, she was desperate to try anything.

"I'll be there," she said. She hugged Chris tight. "Thank you."

❖

The Ivy restaurant on Robertson was a reliable paparazzi hotspot, so it made sense that her agent would choose that establishment to bring Avalon and Garrett Chain together. According to what Billy had told her when he was last at her house, Garrett would be directing a huge production in Spain and was searching for a lead actress. Billy sat between them, referee style, but lacking the whistle and stripes.

She didn't want to appear too anxious for the part, but being too aloof might backfire. Garrett was known as a cautious and mistrustful director, with a great disdain for drama. But she was sure the film would be a blockbuster. She also knew that it was the first of a trilogy, and the contract was not only lucrative, it was lucrative in triplicate.

"*The Last Stand* is doing very well," Billy said over their lunch of an iceberg-wedge salad, no dressing for him, wild swordfish for Garrett, and pasta for her. "They're on budget and schedule, and they wrap in a week."

"And what's the difficulty I'm hearing," Garrett said to Avalon, "about you and Jessica Wiley?"

"No troubles at all, Garrett," Billy quickly said.

She held her hand up to Billy. "It was contentious, yes. But things have died down. I have no desire to have that part of my life in the press."

"One point two million hits on YouTube is hardly keeping that part of your life out of the press."

What's with this muttonhead? Everyone gets bad press. And it sells movies, or does he think his work is above that? "I guarantee you, it's over and done."

"Avalon's doing her own stunts in *The Last Stand*." Changing the subject might just earn Billy his 15 percent commission.

"Risky, isn't it?" Garrett chomped loudly on his swordfish, which rankled her. How could swordfish be loud?

"Not at all," she said before Billy could answer for her. "We have the best stunt director in the business. And my double does the more dangerous stunts."

Garrett chewed for a while. Then he said, "I've seen some of the dailies. You're good."

"Thank you." His chewing was bugging her less.

"How are you with love scenes?"

She lifted her glass of water and took a sip. "The same as I am with any scene. Good."

She wished she could say that about her love life. She'd made a terrible mess of her relationship with Paige, who wasn't answering her phone calls. Her pasta sat untouched because her stomach couldn't handle the effort. She felt literally sick about what had happened at the Chateau Marmont pool. What the hell had she been thinking? She'd grabbed Paige because she wanted to shove the fact that it was over in Jessica's face, but she had been too forceful and…horribly boorish.

She cringed and Garrett looked her way.

A positive outcome to this meeting was extremely important because it held the possibility of her next movie. It would cement her position in Hollywood, and the phrase *with a bullet* would actually be more like *with a rocket missile*.

But the magnitude of it all paled when she compared it to the fact that she'd lost Paige. She wanted the lunch to be over. She had to set things right.

Billy scratched at the floral tablecloth as if he were trying to pick a bouquet of flowers. Maybe that's what she should do. She would send flowers to Paige. No. She would take flowers over.

"I'd like you to read with a few actors," Garrett said.

Billy began to protest but Avalon interrupted. "I'd be happy to."

But not as happy as I could be, she thought morosely. When would lunch be *over*?

❖

"The stage is a magical place." Dee Jae sat in a circle of four others on her small stage in the theater.

Paige adjusted her butt on the metal folding chair, and the wooden slatted floor, aged and worn from decades of thespian traffic, creaked miserably. The place smelled of musty curtains and the slight but dank aroma of cigarettes that had probably been smoked years before, leaving their remnants permanently saturated in the fabric and theater seats. The crisp green scent of newly cut wood was also present, probably emanating from the set walls that lay against the brick wall in back, awaiting a coat of paint. She surveyed the participants, all women, of various ages and body types. All were listening intently and taking notes.

"There's an immediacy with a live audience that film cannot duplicate," Dee Jae said. "So, we're here to create that immediacy and intimacy."

Intimacy was not a word Paige needed to hear right then. Her desire to be as far away from it had propelled her to attend Dee Jae's workshop. She needed to lose herself in something other than Avalon.

Avalon's messages and texts, though, kept hovering around her brain like meddlesome bees insistent on finding sustenance.

Paige, please listen to me. I'm so sorry about what happened.
We need to talk. Please?
Don't give up on us, Paige. I want to work this out.

Paige wasn't sure how to work it all out. Maybe she was being too sensitive about things. People did make mistakes. But she would never act as aggressively and disrespectfully as Avalon had. And the act of aggression concerned her.

Still, it was virtually impossible to erase the feelings for Avalon that had swelled tremendously in her heart.

"...types of plays out there," Dee Jae was saying. "There are ten-minute plays, one-acts, full-length, and musicals. We'll focus on one-act plays. The goal in this workshop will be to write a fifteen- to twenty-minute piece. The plots shouldn't be too complicated. We will have one shared set that you will all be incorporating into your play. I'll determine the set. The goal at the end of this workshop will be to cast and rehearse your play, and then we'll have a showcase. You can invite your friends and family, and we'll advertise. Last year we had a packed house!"

The participants looked at each other with the same nervous but excited expressions. Paige wished she could feel more like them, but the only thing in her gut was a spreading puddle of foul, viscous despondency. For them, this was their chance to break out in Hollywood. For her, this was a necessary distraction.

❖

Parking on the street was more difficult to find than usual, and Paige finally squeezed into a spot over a block away from her apartment.

Since leaving the workshop, she'd been running play ideas through her head. The setting Dee Jae had told them their plays would be constructed around would be a section of Sunset Boulevard in Hollywood. Lots of possibilities ran amok in her head. Homeless people, police officers, and starlet-wannabes could all provide great fodder for her play. They had five weeks to write their work and then cast and rehearse before the showcase. The timing was working out well. She'd be too busy with her screenplay to chew herself up with worry about the book tour, as it was starting right after the showcase.

The gate to her courtyard clanged shut and she walked toward the fountain by her front door. She stiffened when she noticed the silhouette of a darkened figure standing by the door. She stopped. She'd heard too many stories of murders, rapes, and all the big-bad-city crime that could happen on any street no matter how nice or neighborhood-watched.

"Who the fuck are you?" She wanted the upper hand first. If it was someone up to no good, they might think twice about hassling her.

"It's me, Paige." Avalon stepped into the beam of her porch light, holding a magnificent bouquet of flowers.

"Avalon," she said in relief. She looked so good, and a ripple of desire quickly spread through her. Her heart ached as desperately as a castaway glimpsing an approaching ship. She stepped closer.

When she reached her, Avalon said, "Can we talk?"

Two long weeks had passed since that day at the Chateau Marmont. Paige had left the refuge of her apartment a few times, but everywhere she went, magazine stands and radio news shows had announced Avalon's latest goings-on. Even at home, channel surfing became treacherous work because of the coverage Avalon got. And though Paige tried to ignore the gossip, she was aware that Avalon had kept to herself. There were no rumblings of Jessica or any other woman on her arm.

But whatever microscopic amount of strength she'd gained from Avalon's absence immediately melted away when she gazed at those light jade eyes.

She let Avalon into her apartment, though she was still upset and wasn't sure if she could trust what she might say.

Avalon handed her the flowers and she took them with a weak thank you.

"I'm not sure whether you listened to my voice mail messages," Avalon said, "but the summation of all of them is a big I'm sorry."

"I'm sure you are, Avalon. I doubt you'd say that if you weren't. But apologies don't mean much if they keep following new stunts." She paused. At this point, she supposed she had nothing to gain by speaking her mind, except maybe a hundred more nights of staring at her apartment walls...alone. "The second or third time you said 'I'm sorry' makes me believe that there's a pattern, and I don't like that."

Avalon listened and paused as if truly absorbing Paige's words. She nodded slowly, almost reverently. "I'd like us to try again." She stepped closer and took Paige's hand. "To play off the bullshit and focus on the real stuff."

"I don't understand."

"I'm asking you to separate that gossip and paparazzi shit from us. You need to ignore anything that happens in public. It's just BS to sell magazines."

"That's just it." She let go of Avalon's hand and stepped back. "It's not BS. It involved me personally."

"But that's Hollywood. This is what happens here. You sign up for the rodeo and have to deal with the dust that comes with it."

"Dust? You think it's just dust?"

"It's a necessary ingredient. The press creates a buzz, and the buzz creates more magazine sales and movie attendance, and that creates more work."

"It's what happens to cause the buzz. You get into nasty little predicaments and say extreme, embarrassing things. And that day at the pool, I…I didn't know who the hell you were. It was like you turned into a grabby macho idiot."

"And I'm apologizing for all of that, Paige. I don't like it either, but my public life is not my own."

"Don't you see that the way you are in public is just a façade? And you play into that. The Hollywood that the average person thinks they understand is nothing more than a bunch of glossy magazine stories."

"My life is not feed for a bunch of four-dollar rags. Hollywood is my life, Paige."

Paige's simmering frustration bubbled up and elevated the volume of her voice. "Hollywood is your *career*. You do a job, like everyone else. The crazy lifestyle that's attached to it isn't what you're paid to do. It's what you choose to do."

"You don't get it."

"Maybe I don't," she said. "But you're missing my point."

Avalon stopped and took a deep breath. "Paige, your point

is that you're uncomfortable with my behavior when we're in public."

Paige nodded.

"So I'm asking that you give us another chance. Give me the opportunity to show you that we can be in public together without the craziness."

"Aren't you afraid you won't sell magazines that way?" She regretted her question as soon as it left her mouth. Avalon's face flashed to something, but the emotion disappeared so quickly, she couldn't tell whether it was anger, or irritation, or something else.

Whatever it was, Avalon chose to ignore the question. "Can we try?"

A kernel of doubt hovered in her chest, thick with hesitation and worry. When she'd started seeing Avalon, the locomotive of the star's life came barreling down the tracks at her. And now, having faith that the train would change course somehow seemed impractical, at the very least. But one thing that hadn't changed course was the substantial weight of her feelings for Avalon. She'd fallen so hard. And even when she'd hit the proverbial pavement by the Chateau Marmont pool, the impact hadn't jarred one iota of her attraction for Avalon.

"I just don't think I could handle the paparazzi and publicity."

"Let me manage it for us."

"Why manage it at all?" She knew the statement was absurd, but she had come to loathe that aspect of Avalon's life.

"I have to. It's how I keep visible. Fans make or break me."

"What about your work? Isn't that what you're judged on?" She knew her words were biting.

"It's about an image. You should know. You write about Hollywood. And why do you do that?" Avalon's voice escalated. "Because people want to know about it. They expect glamorous, exciting stories. You're a hypocrite because you peddle the same shit that you're complaining about."

"I tell the stories of the movies themselves."

"And the lives of the actors who play in them. It's a whole package."

"Well, I don't know if I want the whole package."

Before she could add that there were parts of the package she very much wanted, Avalon turned and walked away. This very gesture from Avalon, her showing up so humble and willing to try, was one of the parts of her she very much wanted.

Paige lifted the flowers that had been in her hand and rotated the beautiful bouquet. Jewels of deep-blue velvet poppies, orange freesias, yellow trumpets, and red fire lilies nestled together like a treasure of precious gemstones and made her miserable beyond belief.

Why is it so hard to take her back when all I want is that very same thing? She was making the slice of Avalon's life that was undesirable the biggest factor in her decision. *And how big is that slice, really?*

Obviously, she thought in an attempt to defend herself, it was big enough to cause hurt and confusion. Her protection radar had blipped bright warnings more than once. She was crazy about Avalon, but she would inevitably get hurt.

This is for your own good, she thought, and hated her own rational tone as much as if it came from a patronizing preacher.

It was fight-or-flight time, and both choices were shitty. If she stayed and fought, she could get the crap beaten out of her emotions. She might as well tie herself to the back of a train and let it drag her down a hundred miles of track. If she ran, she'd regret killing the chance that whatever was between them might work. And if Avalon moved on and eventually forgot about her, she might as well get in front of that same damn train and just lay herself down.

Yes, no. Stay, go. It was all so fucked up.

CHAPTER FIFTEEN

*C*ut to the Chase* was coming together better than Paige had imagined it would. She'd locked herself in her apartment for the better part of the last three weeks, fingers ablaze, as she cranked out 20,000 words of text, most of it needing trivial editing.

She finalized the images of Bubba and Ricky within the first three days. The contrast between two such different men, in both personality and stature, illustrated the ends of the macho spectrum, proving that Hollywood could make the clumsy appear elegant and the spineless seem brave. While she had a modicum of success in remaining fairly detached while writing about Avalon, editing and cropping the photographs was an entirely different beast. The work slowed to a painful crawl when she finally got to Avalon's photos.

She had to admit they were all spectacular, but each memory-filled image slammed against her with the force of a wrecking ball against a brick building.

When she reached the image she'd taken of Avalon taking a swing at her costar, she was extremely satisfied with the composition. Avalon's body arced like she was throwing a discus, and the energy of that curve carried through to the backward bend of Brent Hastings's body as he reacted to the theatrical blow. It was like a painting that expressed the tremendous forcefulness in one perfect brushstroke. And Avalon's face completed the compelling photograph. A declaration of absolute commitment screamed from her eyes and mouth. Her expression was that of a gambler who goes all in at the high-stakes table, no matter what the outcome.

She'd stared at that picture for hours, it seemed, trying to convince herself that it wasn't the exact same look Avalon had when they'd made love. But it was. Paige had seen that all-inclusive devotion more than once. Her heart ached constantly. She toyed with her cell phone countless times, wanting so desperately to call her, but what would she say?

Avalon's life moved like a rocket, and Paige simply wasn't cut out for that type of trajectory. If they could only run away somewhere where there was no paparazzi, no movies, no fans… but that was tantamount to killing Avalon's livelihood. Paige would never let anyone do that to her photography career.

It just wasn't meant to be, she told herself with each pass of her Photoshop tools as she cleaned up a background blob on Avalon's clothes or softened a shadow across her face.

Finally, however, she was almost ready to submit the pages to Carmen. She'd written the acknowledgments, and the only thing left was the dedication.

The dedication.

In her first book, she'd thanked her college photography professor. The passionate and animated little man who always wore black pants, a crisp white shirt, and slender black suspenders had opened up her world to infinite creative possibilities. Her second book expressed gratitude to her parents. Even though a degree of disappointment in her choice of professions seemed to perfume the air in her parents' house, she thanked them for rearing her and putting her through college. She loved her parents and, after all, had found her calling, no matter how frequently they crooked their eyebrows.

To, she typed. She had many wonderful people in her life

and she could name any one of them, but only one name seemed appropriate.

To Avalon. She deleted that. *To A.R.—for the lovely woman you are inside.*

That sounded so brainless.

She stared at the page on her computer. Then she typed: *To A.R.—the woman I've fallen unbelievably hard for. I can't get you out of my mind and wish every day that things were different. You're the lightest breath on my neck, the warmest arms around my shoulders, the everything I could ever want.*

The weight of a million what-ifs threatened to crumple her. What if she gave Avalon another chance? She hesitated, her finger hovering over the Backspace key like a jumper on the roof of a building. She let her finger fall onto the key, pressed it, and watched the words disappear until it simply read *To A.R.*

She hit Save and sent the manuscript to Carmen.

❖

"Take me home." Avalon's head sloshed around with the woozy effects that alcohol had caused, but not so much that she couldn't realize that agreeing to have dinner with Jessica had been a very bad idea.

"We're right by the Abbey. I want another drink. Just one more." Jessica's three drinks at dinner had already taken effect as she veered over the lane lines on Melrose Avenue.

Avalon grabbed the side armrest. She checked her watch. She'd limited herself to two drinks, and it had been over an hour since her first. "Pull over, Jess."

"Why?"

"Just pull over. I'm driving."

"We're almost there."

Not with the way she was driving. They'd be lucky if they reached anywhere safely. Avalon's stomach tightened in frustration. She didn't want to spend one more minute with her ex.

Over the previous week, Jessica had left a number of polite and apologetic voice mails asking if they could mend their differences, and Avalon had unwisely taken the bait.

With *The Last Stand* now in post-production, Avalon was bombarded with interviews and press coverage, and Billy was in the final stages of negotiations with Garrett, almost ready to ink the deal that would put her in Spain on his film. She was busy and fairly happy, except for one thing. The hole Paige had left in her heart remained tender and sore. Thoughts of her filled every void in her life. She replayed the day at the Chateau Marmont pool so many times that she stayed sick with regret, and as badly as she wanted to mend the pain she'd caused Paige, their last words seemed to cement the finality of their different lives.

She had reluctantly agreed to Jessica's invitation for dinner at Cecconi's, and from the minute they arrived, Jessica had acted like they were back together. Jessica tried to put her arm around her, moved her chair as close to her as possible, leaned in romantically, and laughed way too loud for the actual conversation at hand. The room erupted in buzzing faster than a chain saw cuts through pine. Conversely, every minute with Jessica seemed to pass slower than stalactites form, so Avalon ordered the Italian tapas for both of them because they would be brought to the table faster than dinner.

Jessica managed to down three drinks in that time and hardly absorbed the message of *we're over* that Avalon had peppered the conversation with.

Finally, Avalon said, "Jessica, I'm not sure why you wanted to have dinner, but I can tell you that you're putting on quite a show."

"No, I'm not."

"If you want to officially mend our differences, they're mended, okay? We're not getting back together. I'll be civil with you in public and I want the same."

"Baby, let's just enjoy the evening—"

"I'm not enjoying this. And I want to leave."

"Okay," she said, but it wasn't until Jessica was behind the wheel that Avalon realized how inebriated she was. All the more irritated, she grew incensed when the car lurched every time Jessica turned to talk to her. Not only did she need to get her out of the driver's seat, she intended to drive her home and call herself a cab.

"Pull the fucking car over! I'm going to drive!"

With a few jerks, Jessica managed to get over to a red curb and stop. They switched seats and Avalon pulled back onto Melrose.

When they approached Robertson, Jessica said, "Go to the Abbey. Turn here. Turn here."

"I'm taking you home."

Jessica yelled *What?* and grabbed the steering wheel, tugging it toward the right. Avalon raised her arm to wrench the wheel from Jessica's grip and turned the wheel in the opposite direction. In a split second, the struggle escalated, the car accelerated, and tires screeched. An explosion seemed to break Avalon's eardrums, and something punched her in the face as shattering glass and a sickening crunch of metal brought the car to a stop.

CHAPTER SIXTEEN

Paige collected her stage-play notebook and scooped her keys off the counter. Dee Jae's classes had been her salvation, filling her nights with activities much more productive than ice cream, Oreo cookies, and *I Love Lucy* reruns.

Her cell phone chirped. "Hi, Chris, I'm just on my way out the—"

"Turn your TV on."

"What?"

"Channel Two. It's coming on after the commercial break."

Paige picked up her remote and clicked the television on. "What is?"

"Just watch."

A car commercial ended and *Entertainment Tonight* came on. A picture of Avalon appeared on the screen and host Nancy O'Dell began to speak.

"As we reported before the break, actress Avalon Randolph has just been released from the hospital after a car accident last night that resulted in the total loss of the Aston Martin she was driving. Reports say she was driving erratically and smashed into a brick building on the corner of Melrose and San Vicente. When police arrived, she allegedly fought with them and resisted arrest. A Breathalyzer test registered point zero eight, the bare minimum needed for a DUI. Jessica Wiley, her ex-lover, was also in the car at the time and is reported to own the car. Avalon and Jessica were taken to Cedar Sinai Hospital, where they were treated for their injuries. Avalon was then booked at the nearby Hollywood police station and released earlier this evening."

Paige slowly dropped to the couch. "Shit."

"Yeah," Chris said. "I mean, what the hell?"

It seemed that Avalon was okay, arrest and injuries aside, but what was she doing with Jessica? A sour slab of nausea landed in the bottom of her stomach. Were they back together? She wanted to cry. Yes, she had refused Avalon's white flag, but selfishly, as long as Avalon wasn't dating anyone else, she still held out hope that something might change. Now hopelessness leached though her skin and into her bloodstream, poisoning any chance of love and even staining the memories of their time together. It was truly over, and nothing would help her feel even the slightest bit okay.

She felt the hardness of the car keys in her hand and gripped them tight. Even the sanctuary of Dee Jae's class was gone.

❖

Lawyers. A necessary cog in the wheels of business. The unemotional rescuer of the unlawful.

Avalon sat glumly in a mahogany-paneled office of Stanley Erickson. How many celebrities had contributed to his high-rise view overlooking Century City and the endless maze of thickly carpeted offices and expensive furniture that filled the entire twelfth floor of his renowned plea-bargaining principality?

She shouldn't have gone anywhere with Jessica. It had been stupid to think she could get Jessica to understand that it was over for good. She'd hoped she could close the fissure of contempt between them and end the constant drama. She didn't need that kind of bullshit anymore. That was precisely the part of the package Paige hadn't wanted. And though she'd lost Paige, the least she could do was honor her words and start to act in a way that Paige would be proud of. But she'd accomplished quite the opposite. She'd caused an even bigger scene by crashing the car with her ex. Maybe the part Paige was talking about was impossible to remove.

She'd had a stomachache since the night at Paige's doorstep. Though Paige's words had been the truth, they'd cut her with the devastation of a machete. The deep, ripping pain reminded her of the loving woman she no longer had. Each time she lay down, the sharp sting of loss ground into her like little shards of glass rubbed roughly into her skin. And the realization of how she'd fucked up was like someone pouring alcohol mercilessly into the bloody wound.

"Four months of community service and suspension of your driver's license," Stanley said after reviewing her paperwork for, maybe, two minutes.

"No fucking way," she shouted.

Michele D. rested her hand on Avalon's wrist. "Is that the best you can do?"

Avalon didn't even try to stop her knee from bouncing in frustration. "Christ…"

Stanley looked up from his papers. "I'm not selling you a used car, Ms. Randolph. The *best I can do* is what I can convince the DA of. You'll be responsible for restitution to both the car and the building. You have priors, I see, for disorderly conduct. That doesn't help. With the recent publicity around some celebrities, the days of light sentences are quickly coming to an end."

The day before, the charges read at the arraignment were like sharp whacks from a wooden paddle: DUI, resisting arrest, property damage auto, property damage structure. After her plea of not guilty, the judge ordered her free on bail, which she immediately paid. Michele D. picked her up, told her she'd set up a meeting with Erickson, and dropped her off at home.

With stomach-turning clarity, she remembered the whole

night: the crash, the scuffle with the police, the hospital visit, and the police station. Most upsetting was her confrontation with the West Hollywood PD. She was so enraged at Jessica and then so spun up by the crash, she'd taken it out on them. Her mouth had spouted foolish and rash bullshit like the cops were the paparazzi. But they weren't. And with an abrupt clank of handcuffs, her goose had been cooked.

All this because she had agreed to dinner with Jessica. She touched her split lip, running her fingers lightly over the four stitches that still hurt quite a bit. She had burned her hand on the chemicals from the airbag when it had exploded, and the bruise that traveled from her shoulder down past her collarbone was tender, but that was the extent of her injuries. Community service would be publicly embarrassing, but it wasn't horrible. Even though Jessica was far drunker, Avalon had gotten behind the wheel and crashed the car. She had to step up and take that responsibility. Losing her license would also be incredibly inconvenient, but she could hire a driver. Anything was better than jail time.

"Fine," she said. "When does this all start?"

"We'll see at your preliminary hearing. I'll talk to the DA and see if we can settle on a plea."

She turned to Michele D. "At least I've got Garrett Chain's film to look forward to. Do you think they'll let me go to Spain in the middle of all this?"

Michele D.'s face seemed to pale instantly.

Avalon's stomach lurched. "What?"

Michele D. spoke to Erickson. "Are we done here?"

He nodded and, as she stood, Avalon did the same.

"What, Michele?"

Without another word, Michele walked out, and all Avalon could do was will her now-shaking legs to follow.

❖

Michele sat in her car with her cell phone in the palm of her hand. The speakerphone made her agent, Billy, sound like a nervous cricket in tall grass.

"Garrett's already gotten wind of this, Avalon," he said. "We're out of the negotiations."

"Are you fucking serious?"

"He says you're too much of a risk to production."

"When have I ever missed a day of work?"

"We need to set up a meeting with Garrett," Michele D. said.

"He's got to be"—Avalon began to say, and when Michele D. raised her hand, Avalon slapped it away—"kidding!"

"I already asked. He said no."

"I'm the best choice for this. The top choice."

"I know," Billy said. "But he's adamant."

"He's an ass." Avalon's head was throbbing in turmoil. "What are our options, Billy?"

The protracted pause screamed in Avalon's ears.

"Nothing. We're out."

"Shit." She needed aspirin badly.

"Until this washes over," Michele D. looked dangerously stern, "you need to stay out of the press. I don't want you talking to anyone."

"This is when the paparazzi will be at its nosiest. They'll be relentless," Avalon said.

"And you don't say a word, do you understand? No comments about how unfair this all is or that it happens to a lot of stars. If you're seen out, go about your business without opening your mouth."

She shook her head, disbelief making it pound so loudly she could hear the thumping of her heart.

"I'm canceling all interviews, as well. I don't want anyone thinking about you at all."

"Fuck." Avalon's frustration boiled inside. That was tantamount to death.

CHAPTER SEVENTEEN

Frenetic colored lights raced around Avalon's peripheral vision like bees swarming around a huge hive, and deafening music pounded so loudly, her chest rumbled. Long ago, it seemed, she had cared who saw her sitting at the Effen bar in the Abbey, but now she wanted desperately to be invisible. She hunched over her fourth or maybe fifth glass of vodka, ignoring the steady influx of stargazing, hopeful women who sidled up next to her, only to leave after realizing she wouldn't look up and acknowledge them.

Fuck this bar, she thought. *Fuck these women.*

Her cell phone buzzed again and she ignored that as well. It was either Michele D. or Billy, two nuisances who were now each earning 15 percent of zero dollars to harangue her into cleaning up her act.

Headlines from magazines and images from entertainment shows stomped around in her brain like schizophrenic voices—relentless and unyielding.

"Avalon Randolph's fall from grace…"

"Another celebrity scandal that has surprised no one…"

"She can't get a job, no one will hire the out-of-control actress…"

"Disorderly, disruptive, and dissed by Hollywood…"

The press had had a field day with her. She was suddenly a

pariah in the eyes of the producers and directors in town. No one would return her calls. The global reaction had been ridiculous because many celebrities had been in the same predicament at one time or another—some even seeing their career change for the better afterward. But the previous bad press had been mounting, and then the car accident, coupled with Garrett's very public rejection of her, had created the perfect storm. It didn't help that it had all happened in an otherwise slow few weeks for the press. The sharks had ripped at her flesh, hungry for anything they could tear off and feast on.

She emptied her glass and pounded it on the bar top.

"No more for you, okay?"

She lifted her head. The face of the bartender was swirling like a 60s psychedelic light show of oil and water.

"Fine," she replied, and tried to stand up. She fell against the woman sitting next to her, then pushed away, only to sway in the opposite direction, landing against two other women, who caught her in their arms.

She said excuse me, but thought the words could have come out as a grunt and began to scramble toward the bar's entrance. She knew people were looking and she assumed others had their cell phones out, documenting her drunken state, but she didn't fucking care.

Someone called her name, but she focused on the streetlights at the sidewalk. Suddenly, she tripped on something and landed hard on her knee. Hands grabbed her under her arms and lifted her up. She shoved them away, staggered on, and finally grabbed the ironwork fence at the entrance.

A taxi had pulled away and she swore out loud. "Where's a fucking cab, where's a fucking cab," she repeated to herself.

"Want a ride home?"

She turned to see a tall butch woman whom she didn't know.

"No."

"Come on, let me get you home," the woman said, and stepped closer.

Another cab pulled up to the curb and she reached for the door. It wouldn't open right away, and she fought with the handle until it flipped up and she was finally able to fall inside.

As she closed the door, the butch woman yelled, "You're a mess, anyway."

❖

Paige had what seemed to be a nonstop series of nightmares, all around public speaking. Unnerving and distressing scenarios pummeled her as she thrashed and tried to cry out in her nocturnal paralysis. In her last one, she dreamt that she was in front of hundreds of book buyers at a signing event where she was to speak about *Cut to the Chase*. She opened her mouth and nothing came out. As the crowd grew angry, her heart began to race. Suddenly the readers were yelling and throwing her books. She dodged as many as she could, but the onslaught was too formidable. Her heart was now pounding so ferociously she could hear it banging against her chest.

Bang, bang—the beat of her heart became deafening.

The crowd turned into villagers carrying torches, chanting, "Talk! Talk!"

Bang, bang—she could feel her pumping organ begin to explode.

She suddenly opened her eyes and lay still in bed.

Bang, bang.

It was the front door.

She jumped up, alarmed. Trotting over, she opened the door quickly, afraid the apartment complex was on fire.

Avalon stood there, disheveled and drunk.

"What are you doing here?" Paige shook the rest of the sleep from her brain.

Garish streaks of black mascara ran down Avalon's cheeks. "Can I come in?"

Paige took her hand and pulled her in. Avalon almost fell and Paige grabbed her, helping her to the couch.

"I'm so sorry," Avalon said. "Everything's so fucked up. I fucked us up, too."

"Now's not the time to talk." The clock read three a.m. She pulled a blanket from the back of the couch. "Here," she said as she helped Avalon lie down, which was quite easy since she seemed to crumple at her touch. She spread the blanket over her and Avalon whimpered.

"Do you need a garbage can close by?"

"Maybe…"

Paige carried a can over and left her with a washcloth and a glass of water. "Just go to sleep, okay?"

Paige walked to her room, and as she crossed the threshold, she heard a weak murmur.

"I love you."

She turned back toward the couch but couldn't see Avalon, who was slumped on the cushions on the other side. She began to walk back but stopped. *Don't give that any weight*, she told herself. *She's drunk and probably feeling lost and lonely. Sleep is what she needs.*

Now wide-awake, she climbed back into bed.

In the weeks since she'd turned Avalon away at her door, she'd followed the press's account of Avalon's descent. Numerous drunken nights and scathing photos flooded all news outlets like candy from a piñata. She'd wanted to call her so many times, to tell her she cared so much for her and to offer encouragement, but each time, she hesitated. As much as she wanted to see her again and let her know she loved her, what good would it do? She couldn't keep up in Avalon's world of high-speed commotion.

But here she was, asleep on her couch. She hadn't gone to one of her, probably, hundreds of friends. She'd come to her house. That had to mean something, didn't it?

How she wished things were different. A Tasmanian devil of a woman had swirled into her life, and as strong as her dream was to chase tornados, this one seemed way too perilous.

She stared through the doorway, to the couch where one of Hollywood's celebrities was passed out.

Just see what happens in the morning, she told herself.

With Avalon only a room away, Paige could picture her stretched out on the couch. She could feel Avalon's lips and mouth and the weight of her body. The sensations of tasting her and being inside her tormented Paige to the point of frustration. She shook from deep inside. Avalon lay so close by, and Paige couldn't rub away or shake off her little tremors of apprehension and angst. Paige could no more control her shivering than if she were naked in the Arctic. The deep, emotional chills that shook her body were annoying and utterly maddening. *Close your eyes and get some sleep.* But the images and sensory recollections of Avalon forced slumber to dance teasingly just out of her reach.

CHAPTER EIGHTEEN

Paige wrapped herself in a robe and tiptoed out of her bedroom. From the back of the couch, she could see part of the blanket that Avalon must have thrown off. Her chest felt heavy from staying up all night fighting to exorcise the sexy thoughts and feelings of Avalon that had possessed her. They'd swirled inside, refusing to leave. She'd spent the night crawling through a cryptograph full of riddles about jumbled logic and reason and conundrums of feelings and desire.

It took all night to break the code, but now she knew what it meant.

She loved her. She sighed at her predicament and went to the kitchen, put on a pot of coffee, and let her butt rest against the counter.

What would today bring that would be any different from the days before? Avalon was a mess. Hollywood was gossiping that her uncontrollable behavior was too much of a gamble for the director of a blockbuster movie to risk investing in.

There had been too many pictures of a drunk and disheveled Avalon floating around the Internet, so Paige stayed away and focused on her book.

Now that *Cut to the Chase* was in her publisher's hands, she had a one-act play to finish but not much else to keep her mind off the upcoming and dreadfully frightening book tour and her frustratingly enduring feelings for Avalon.

"Paige?" A weak voice came from the couch.

She poured two cups of black coffee and made her way to the couch. Avalon sat up slowly, making room for her.

"Good morning." Paige handed her a mug and sat. "How are you feeling?"

"Like I gargled with a dead possum."

"That bad, huh?"

"I've been worse." She lowered her head, rubbing her forehead. "I lied. This is the worst."

"How did you get here last night?"

"Taxi."

"I'm glad you didn't drive."

"I can't. My license was suspended."

The way Avalon carefully stood reminded Paige of a ninety-five-year-old lady.

"Do you mind if I take a shower?"

Paige gave her a towel and some sweats and a T-shirt. Avalon's attempt at a smile looked painful. She imagined it was from the hangover, not the discontent she herself felt at the sad realization that they'd probably never get to shower together.

And that made her feel as alone as an untethered astronaut floating away from the comfort of the space capsule.

❖

Thirty minutes later, Avalon emerged from the bathroom feeling much better. The sweats felt comfortable and her hair was wet but clean. She found Paige in the kitchen and was offered some toast. Her stomach felt a little queasy because she'd skipped lunch and dinner the night before, prior to her imbibing. Maybe some carbs would soak up the sourness.

"You were making noises in your sleep last night," Avalon said as she watched Paige spread blackberry jam on the toast.

"Noises?"

"Talking, almost yelling. Like you were having trouble."

Paige handed her a plate and put her own on the counter. As she took a seat on one of the bar stools, Avalon did the same.

"Nightmares," Paige said. "The book tour."

"That bad, huh?"

"I'm not looking forward to it, if you want to know the understated truth. More coffee?"

"No, thank you. One cup is enough." She tore a piece of toast and chewed it tentatively, in case her stomach had nefarious ideas. The sweet, full flavor of the blackberries was superb.

"How's your head?"

"Okay. Maybe that means I've gotten used to the alcohol."

Paige looked at her dubiously. "What's going on, Avalon?"

She smirked at the obvious, as if being asked whether pancakes were cakes you made in a pan. "Drowning my sorrows, I suppose."

"Do you want to know what I think?"

She kind of didn't because she knew it would probably be the truth. "I do."

"Those emotional bruises you're feeling? They're from falling off the mountain of hype you built for yourself. You kept making it bigger and bigger, and then one day, splat, you fell off."

"I can't argue with that."

"So who are you without the mountain? Who are you without the movies, your manager, agent, or your fans?"

It had been so long, she didn't know.

"And where did you cross that line of acceptable behavior? It's like the paparazzi raise their cameras and you're granted free license to be an ass."

"Ouch." She found herself more humbled than she'd ever been, and for once, she didn't fight it. Maybe it was the hangover or maybe this woman had finally gotten through to her. "You're right."

"I'm not trying to be mean, Avalon."

"I know you aren't." A sobering realization brought an

empty laugh to her lips. "You're one of the few people who are truly honest with me." She hung her head, ashamed of where she'd ended up. She was responsible for her predicament, no one else. "I didn't pay attention when I started to lose myself. I willingly drank the Kool-Aid, but somewhere along the way, my spirit drained and then there was just this hollow vessel.

"Michele D., my manager, warned me about going off the rails again." Avalon rubbed at the beginnings of an ache in her head as the truth of her behavior became increasingly clear. "When I first broke up with Jessica, I didn't handle that well, either. She helped by pushing my buttons at the right times, like when we were in public, but the bad behavior was all me. The press just ate it up. And then I was stupid enough to accept a 'truce' dinner with her. I should have known it would go all wrong."

"It wasn't a reconciliation dinner?"

"Oh, my God, no. I hoped we could end our stupid squabbling and agree to be civil." She shook her head slowly. "What a mess. But I've also been told I can't talk to the press for a while."

"Who told you that?"

"My manager. I've been gagged."

"You can't even respond to whatever they're saying?"

"No. I suppose Michele D. doesn't trust me and my mouth. I can't disagree with her, but it's hard not defending myself. And it seems the press wants to talk about me a lot these days."

"I looked up the word *celebrity* online," Paige said. "Do you know what it said? Something like, celebrity is the sole manifestation of the public's sense of upward mobility and illusions of wealth that they, too, might obtain for themselves."

"The American dream," Avalon said, feeling rather foolish. Fame was as fleeting and fickle as a soap bubble.

"Holding up the American dream for all mankind is a pretty lofty burden."

The sarcasm didn't escape her. "Well, as you can see, I haven't really been doing a good job of it lately."

Normally the subsequent silence, like the one that followed

a negative observation, would make her quickly fill the void with another topic of conversation. It was an obtuse diversion meant to avoid the palpable reality of her shortcomings. The stillness felt like a theater klieg light, drowning out all other details except for the pool that it illuminated. But this time, she lingered in the stinky, marshy discomfort of her predicament. Paige didn't need to hammer it into her, and mercifully she hadn't.

As they both ate their toast and sipped coffee, Paige looked out the front window and, while Avalon couldn't read her thoughts, she imagined there was a bit of deliberation going on.

Who could blame her? Avalon knew her world was a roller coaster and that Paige wasn't used to the accelerated g-forces that it pulled.

She'd been extremely considerate to let her in the night before when probably everything was telling her to slam the door in Avalon's face. But it was possible that the attraction that drove her to seek refuge with Paige was the same force that compelled Paige to let her in.

"Thank you for opening your door last night."

Paige nodded and Avalon wanted to kiss her sleepy face. Still, she didn't want to wear out her welcome.

"I'd better get dressed and get out of your hair." She picked up her dish and mug and placed them in the sink. She approached Paige, who had followed her. "I can't thank you enough for helping me."

And almost unpredictably, they hugged. Paige could have leaned in first, but she wasn't sure. They'd just moved toward each other and the closeness turned her legs into butter.

When they broke the hug, Paige said, "You know, you look much better than you did last night. I don't know how you do it. If I'd been that drunk, I'd look like a dug-up corpse."

"It's not the kind of skill one should be proud of." Avalon held out her hand. She took it without saying a word and followed her to the couch.

"There are four steps to stage fright," Avalon said.

The change in topic, especially to that one, surprised Paige.

"Remember RSUA," Avalon said. "That stands for relax, stop negative talk, use coping statements, and acknowledge your feelings."

"What—"

"Don't interrupt the teacher. Now, the way to relax, this is the *R* part, is to take slow, deep breaths in and out. Four times. This counteracts the feeling that you can't breathe because, in fact, anxiety can make you take in too much oxygen."

She nodded.

"Okay, we're going to try it."

She followed Avalon's lead, looking in her eyes and mimicking her breathing.

"Good," Avalon said. "Second, you have to stop the emergency message looping over and over in your brain that's trying to tell you you're in danger—the *S* part. The people you're speaking in front of aren't scary. Tell your head to stop!"

"Okay."

"I'm waiting."

"Stop!" she yelled.

"That was good." Avalon chuckled. "But to avoid scaring your audience, it's better to use your inside voice."

She laughed. "Got it!"

"Try it again." Avalon waited a moment, then said, "How'd that feel?"

"Good. I said, 'Fuck you, fear.'"

"Nice! Next is the *U* part, to use coping statements. This replaces the negative loop in your head. Things like, *This is easy. I am fine. Everything's great.*"

"My inside voice?"

"Either is fine since you're not yelling out loud." Avalon's smile was endearing.

"I'm great. I'm fine. I can do this. This will be fun."

"That's good!"

"The last one, *A*, is to acknowledge your feelings. Give them a break. Say something like, 'I'm scared but I am okay. Speaking in front of people makes my heart pound but it's really healthy.'"

Avalon lifted her chin. "Your turn."

"I'm gonna shit in my pants but I have another pair with me."

Avalon burst into laughter. "You've got it!"

This was the first time Paige had ever laughed at her fear. And it felt great. "RSUA, I'll remember that."

"I'm glad." Avalon stood. "For that and for the couch last night. Thank you."

"Do you need a ride home?"

"No, I'll take a cab." Avalon walked to the door. "It's like a limo, only cheaper."

She watched Avalon leave, a bundle of happy and sad feelings rolling around inside her. What would Avalon do next? Would she continue to party and collide with the press, or would she maybe slow down and get her life back on track? Her misconduct certainly wasn't the worst Hollywood had seen. And she had to have lawyers and managers doing damage control for her. It was only a matter of time before people would forget and things would get back to normal. Well, not normal—it was Hollywood, after all—but back to the customary ways of Tinseltown.

It was truly ridiculous that an industry that pushed their subjects to their limits would turn on them when they broke. Stories of actresses being told they weren't skinny enough, pretty enough, or talented enough were numerous, and the criticisms struck with brutal force. And all the while, that same industry waited for the fallout, even craved it—with cameras, no less.

Where previously Avalon had been outspoken at every turn, her manager had now rendered her silent in her disgrace and shame. This was the one time Avalon was saying *Fuck you all* with her inside voice, when she should be using her outside voice.

"Oh, my God, yes!" Paige jumped to her feet, almost knocking over the coffee table, and ran to her desk.

CHAPTER NINETEEN

Tawnya picked up Avalon's call right away. "Your ears must have been ringing. I was just about to call you."

Avalon closed her eyes, letting the sound of Tawnya's voice soothe her in the way honey calms a sore throat. "Hi."

"Are you okay?"

"Not really," Avalon said as she sat on the couch, hanging her head. "I take it you've heard."

"About the car accident or that you didn't get the Garrett Chain film?"

"Both."

"I also get that you're punishing yourself quite a bit nowadays."

"Just hanging out with my friends Jack and Jim."

"You forgot Jose. Do you really want to roll like that?"

Avalon felt a pounding in her head. Its cadence was like a drum beating out a warning of impending doom—war drums setting the pace for an upcoming confrontation. And it was painfully obvious that the clash would end in her own complete failure. She lifted her hand to her forehead to stifle the thumping. "I've made a mess of things."

"Yeah."

"Do you have to be so honest?"

"What do you want? Coddling? I don't coddle."

"No." The last wisps of her hangover lingered like persistent bits of jalapeño in her stomach. She needed to stop partying. Her drinking had become a lone undertaking, a million miles from responsible behavior. "I know it's up to me to turn this around."

"It is, sweetie."

"I called," Avalon said, knowing if she asked the question, she'd be truly committed, "to ask you…"

Tawnya remained silent. Why couldn't she change the subject or tell her she'd be okay no matter what? She rubbed her forehead harder because she would be okay, no matter what.

"I wanted to know if the thing in West Hollywood, at the park, is still happening."

"Every week. Seven o'clock."

❖

Avalon stepped into the large room in Plummer Park. Though it was her first time, she recognized a number of people sitting in the semicircle of chairs. Some smiled or waved as she took a seat. The Alcoholics Anonymous meeting in West Hollywood was the safest of meetings to attend. It was not only a mostly gay and lesbian group, it was where many celebrities went to avoid unwanted pomp and circumstance. While all meetings were supposed to be completely anonymous, stories of movie-star outings were common. Here, though, the crowd behaved with the same nonchalance as they did at the gay bars. Straight celebrities attended for that reason and were welcomed with respect and confidentiality.

She didn't think anyone was surprised to see her there, nor was she surprised to see anyone else. The group included extremely affluent attendees—probably bankers, doctors, and new-money people—as well as everyday working folks, all struggling with their demons.

The meeting started and she took a deep, humble breath. It was time for her to face hers. It was beyond time, actually. She initially felt anger and frustration in her gut when she stepped into the meeting room. She hated *having* to do things. Even if she had made the decision, she was telling herself to do something she didn't really want to do, and that would piss her off. Since she'd become a success in Hollywood, she'd done whatever she wanted. No one told her what to do. Yes, Michele D. did, but that was akin to a police officer pulling you over and telling you to slow down. You drove carefully for the next few miles, even for the rest of the day, but you forgot the scolding before long. And walking into a meeting where everyone would be humble and obedient made her squirm with disdain.

And then she remembered the way Paige's face had contorted when Avalon had grabbed her and said those horrible things at the Chateau Marmont. She'd been terrible and hurt Paige in the process. The sobering thought made her nauseous. She'd acted the way she'd wanted and it was utterly disgraceful.

She felt humiliated at her own actions. And then it hit her. That's what she was really feeling about being at the AA meeting. Under all that rebellion lay a thick, uncomfortable blanket of shame. Alcohol wasn't any better a tool for handling her life than her fast and tempestuous mouth. And all the talk of how booze could numb you was actually bullshit. It only intensified the wretched sadness she felt about the demise of her relationship with Paige. It exaggerated the emptiness and magnified the moments of her worst behavior. The headaches and general misery the next mornings also appeased the part of her that needed to feel some punishment.

But it was no way to conduct her life. She imagined herself at fifty, still drinking and fucking things up. Closing her eyes, she pictured how haggard her face would become and how sunken her eyes would look. She would be exhausted and sickly, and her outlook would be darker than the black coffee she'd need every morning just to function. She would become exactly like every gaunt, soulless woman who ambled up and down the seedy part of Sunset Boulevard, looking for her next score.

Avalon shivered as a wave of fear soaked her. It was sudden and dreadful, painfully twisting her stomach as the possibility that continuing her reckless behavior would eventually, and most assuredly, lead to a series of wretched, black days full of dread and lament. That is, if she lived that long. And even if she did, it certainly wouldn't be with Paige.

She felt drained and weary. And she was here, sitting on a cold, hard fold-up chair because she had created her predicament. She alone had conjured up the tempest that had brought her current devastation. That was why she needed to grow all of the ingredients to a humble pie, bake it, eat it, and then fix her shit.

❖

Everyone was animated in Dee Jae's last workshop prior to casting. They'd read and reread their one-act plays aloud and helped each other polish their pieces. Over the weeks, each play had become so familiar that everyone spoke of them as if they were keeping up with growing children.

Paige sat in the semicircle, rapidly tapping her foot on the floor. She was about to tell everyone she'd left her child at the fire station under the Safe Surrender Baby Law.

Dee Jae began the meeting. "I think everyone's plays are reading brilliantly. I've arranged a number of actors and actresses to attend our casting session next week. Many can be in multiple plays so don't worry about someone stealing your first choice."

Paige sheepishly raised her hand. "I know this is a bad time to do this, and don't get mad, but I've scrapped my play for this one." She held up a manuscript like a white flag.

Dee Jae's expression went blank. She could have been confused, shocked, or even pissed. Paige couldn't tell. She quickly handed her the play and Dee Jae opened it to the first page, to the synopsis. Many of the writers froze, transfixed in their preceding movements, waiting for a reaction. Dee Jae remained completely motionless, except her eyes, which darted back and forth like a pendulum on amphetamines.

Paige's foot fidgeted uncontrollably; the suspense was almost unbearable.

Dee Jae finally looked up. "Are you freakin' serious?"

She nodded.

"Shit."

❖

Avalon paced back and forth in her front room, which seemed odd to her, because Billy, who was on the couch, was usually the one who paced. But she was a bundle of raw nerves, and with everything riding on the call they waited for, her entire body refused to be still.

Michele D. sat on an easy chair in the corner, flipping her Montblanc pen between her fingers. The sun coming through the picture window caught the metal, bouncing reflections of silvery flashes on the walls.

"He knows you've been going to AA meetings," Billy said. "He's got to think you're working on yourself."

"And a copy of the story about it that I talked *Entertainment Tonight* into running was sent to his office. With flowers," Michele D. added. "From you personally."

It wasn't, of course. Michele could forge Avalon's name and even a short note, which she had.

Billy's cell phone rang and they all jumped. He punched the button. "Billy Woods. Yes, I'll hold." He looked up and nodded. "Garrett. Hello!"

Michele D.'s pen stopped moving. Avalon stopped pacing and stood with her back to the picture window. The sun on her shoulders felt comforting and reassuring, like it was restoring her well-being. She prayed it wasn't the only redemption she'd receive that day.

"Yes," Billy said, but his expression revealed nothing. "Yes. Of course. Definitely."

What was with all the short responses? Garrett must be chiding him or, at the very least, lecturing him on his Victorian sensibilities. As much as she wanted the movie, and as much as Billy and Michele D. had worked on her behalf, she was dubious about her ability to work side by side with Garrett Chain on a forty- or forty-five-day shooting schedule. But it was time to put on her big-girl panties, cut the bad-behavior shit, and act more professionally.

She'd do whatever it took.

"Uh-huh," Billy said. "Yes. Certainly. I understand."

Finally, when her climaxing anticipation nearly drove her to throw a pillow in his direction, he said thank you and hung up.

Michele D. spoke first. "Was it a yes?"

"Not exactly."

"What the fuck did he say?" Avalon's head churned toward an explosion.

"He wants to meet with you first."

She blew out a breath. "Okay."

"He's not available until next week, but he said to pick a day and time after that, and we'll arrange it with his office."

After Michele D. and Billy left, Avalon felt an unsatisfied modicum of victory. He still wanted to meet, which didn't mean a yes but a maybe. She'd have to convince him she was stable and reliable.

She'd read the script when Billy was still in negotiations with Garrett's production company, and the absurd thing was, the character they were considering her for was everything Garrett loathed in real life. The character was boisterous, unlawful, and incorrigible. So why was he so dogmatic about her?

She suddenly longed to see Paige. At the thought, she inhaled deeply, filling her lungs with air much fresher than the hot air Garrett spewed. Most of her thoughts, no matter how diverse or unrelated, captured her attention only briefly before falling away to what her heart wanted most. Paige was like a welcome non sequitur punching through everything else, like a siren screaming down a busy boulevard.

Today, she really wanted to see her.

❖

Paige juggled two armfuls of groceries as she made her way down the path to her apartment. Up ahead, she could see a group of people and wondered what her neighbors were up to. It was too early for one of their impromptu barbeques.

"Paige!" One person suddenly turned toward her; however, she didn't recognize him at all.

The other four men turned as well and quickly lifted cameras to their faces.

"How's Avalon?"

"Is she still partying?"

Paige clutched the grocery bags.

"No one's seen her out lately. Is she staying with you?"

She retreated back down the path, reaching her car and throwing the bags in before they caught up with her.

"Shit, shit, shit."

Thankfully, Chris was home. She knocked on the door, looking over her shoulder for anyone with a camera. They'd obviously given up because no one looked her way except an old man walking his Chihuahua.

"Bearing gifts?" Chris said when she opened the door.

"Not really." Paige pushed by her and put the bags on Chris's counter. "The ice cream's probably half-melted."

"What's going on?"

"The paparazzi were camped out at my front door. I ran away and came straight here."

"No kidding!"

She removed the ice cream and put it in Chris's freezer. Chris peeked into the other bag, pulled out a bunch of bananas, and helped herself.

"They said Avalon's been missing in action and somehow figured out where I live."

"Have you seen her?"

She told Chris about the night Avalon had showed up at her door and the ensuing conversations, but that she hadn't talked to her since.

"What do you think's happening with her?"

"I'm not sure."

"Then why don't you call her?"

"I'm going to. Today, actually. I have some news for her."

"And that would be…?"

"It's my little secret. For now, at least."

"It doesn't have anything to do with requiring a penicillin shot, does it?"

Paige slapped her arm. "No, you dirty bird." She plucked another banana from the bunch and peeled it back. "God, I'm crazy about her."

"Tell me something I don't know."

Paige bit into the fruit. "She was so sweet to talk to me about speaking in public. She just volunteered the help, and I could tell she didn't want anything in return."

"Underneath it all, Avalon's simply a normal person who understood you and reached out to help."

"Yeah." Her thoughts floated toward Avalon's arms and how wonderful they felt around her. She could still remember the velvety softness of her skin. Chris was right. Underneath it all, she was just like her.

❖

The music swelled to frenetic levels, the trumpets and violins etching sharp notes of terror as a young Steve McQueen pulled his friends out of a movie theater.

When his friend asked what was going on, he told them that something inside the rock they'd found could wipe out their entire town. He'd seen it kill Dr. Hallen, which meant it could kill other people, too.

After the obligatory swell of melodramatic music, he told his friends that they had to find the thing, and with all the teenage angst that he could squeeze from his face, he vowed to make the adults believe them.

Avalon sat curled up on her couch watching the black-and-white film she'd seen at least twenty times before. She could recite almost every line of *The Blob*.

She wished Paige could be sitting here next to her. It was a film she knew as well. They'd point out gaffes together, laugh at the melodramatic acting, and kiss each other. A lot.

As the teenagers activated the town's air-raid horn, Avalon picked up her cell phone and fingered the buttons. Would Paige consider coming over and watching *The Blob* with her? Could they take another try at the relationship? This time, Avalon would keep her protected from all the bad that Hollywood unleashed. She'd show her that she was changing, getting better. Could she make Paige believe her?

Her hand buzzed suddenly and she looked down. The letters that glowed on her screen read *Paige Cornish*. Her heart jump-started to a brisk beat.

"Paige?"

"Hi, Avalon. How are you?"

"Great, now. You're not going to believe what I'm watching right this minute."

"Give me a clue."

She hadn't simply said, *What?* She was right back to their B-movie conversation. Avalon closed her eyes, adoring Paige. "Phoenixville, Pennsylvania. Steve McQueen."

"I wouldn't give much for their chances, running around in the middle of the night, looking for something that might kill them if they found them."

She knew the lines, too! "You're amazing."

"I have a knack for schmaltzy dialogue."

"No, I mean you're amazing all around. I miss you."

There was a pause on the other end. Then Paige's voice came, as soft as down feathers. "I miss you, too." She uttered a velvety moan, like the kind that punctuates a certain truth. "I have something I'd like to ask you."

"Yes to whatever it is."

Paige chuckled. "You might want to reserve your answer until I tell you everything."

"Okay, but I'll still say yes."

"Can you meet me at a theater? It's run by my friend, Dee Jae. I'll text you the address."

"Sure. When?"

"How's tonight? Seven?"

"I'll be there."

Avalon hung up and held the phone to her chest. Her heart felt light and heavy at the same time. Maybe that's what life was supposed to feel like—that all the bad things and all the good things had to have equal time or the balance would be off. Accepting the weight of her past was a way to appreciate the lightness of her present.

She pressed some keys on her phone.

"Mom," she said when she heard the voice that always took her back to her childhood.

"Honey, are you all right?"

"Yes, Mom. I'm fine." Avalon shifted the phone to her other ear. "Well, I haven't been great, but I'm working on things."

"I worry about you, you know."

"I know you do. Listen, I wanted to tell you that I know it wasn't easy to raise me. You fought with me every inch of the way. And I want to thank you for everything you did."

A pause on the other end of the line told Avalon that her mother was searching for the best, most poised response. Triple Ps, of course.

"Thank you, Avalon." There was a slight catch in her voice, as if she was trying to control an emotional moment. Avalon empathized with her. She knew well how laborious it was to staunch any behavior that might taint one's perfect manners.

"Don't worry about me, Mom. I'm fixing things in my life. I…I just wanted you to know."

"You're a strong woman, Avalon. I would never have expected any less from you."

"I love you."

"I love you, too, dear."

❖

When Dee Jae rearranged the chairs for the third time, Paige held up her hand. "Stop, already."

Dee Jae froze as if being flashed with *Men In Black*'s neuralizer.

"Just calm down," Paige said. "I don't want Avalon to think you're a maniac."

Dee Jae's shoulders dropped in submission. "But I am, kinda. And she's so…famous! I've never had an A-list player in my theater before. Lots of Bs and Cs, and some As in the audience, but no As in the—"

"Just sit down and chill."

Dee Jae sat down, but her fingers rapped a furious staccato on her knees.

"Do you think she'll do this?"

"I hope so."

"Oh, my God. I've got to send word out much further and faster than I have. The place will be packed."

"If she agrees," Paige said, and truly wasn't sure.

The stage side door opened and Avalon walked in. Dee Jae

launched off the chair and skidded up to her. "Avalon, I'm Dee Jae. You must be Avalon!"

Avalon laughed and held out her hand. Dee Jae took it and seemed to dissolve where she stood. Paige came over and took Avalon's other hand. "Come on, let's sit down."

She gave Avalon a set of pages. Dee Jae already had the script. "Dee Jae produces and directs workshops for aspiring screenwriters."

Avalon looked at her with the eyes of a playful sprite. "Screenwriting, huh?"

"I may have *A Streetcar Named Desire* in me."

"Of that I have no doubt."

She now looked at her with such…what? Affection? Love? Paige fought the desire to move to her and kiss her. If Dee Jae hadn't been there, she would have, without reservation. She'd straddle her in the chair and take her face in her hands. They'd kiss softly, at first, until she felt Avalon move her hips, pushing up to tell her she wanted her, too.

The clearing of a throat brought her out of her musings.

"That's my one-act play." Paige pointed to the script that Avalon held. "And all of us in the workshop are going to participate in a showcase where the plays will be performed."

"And you want me to act in the showcase?"

Paige held her breath. "Yes."

"*Underneath It All*," Avalon said, reading the title.

Paige watched her open the script and begin to read. Out of the corner of her eye, she could see Dee Jae drumming her fingers on her knees again.

Avalon's face read like a cartoon flip book as her smile ratcheted down in measured steps as she continued reading. *Shit.* She didn't like it.

Paige began to say something but told herself to just let her finish the play. A muffled door slammed somewhere in the building, as if someone was smart enough to flee the scene. As she sat there, nervous and expectant, the musty aroma from the stage curtains and the smell of well-oiled wood intensified, as if a resident thespian ghost was swirling up the atmosphere. It became stifling. Dee Jae's fingers escalated into a fully sustained legato.

Avalon finally looked up. "Is this for real?"

"Yes." Paige struggled, needing to clear her throat of the angst and apprehension lodged there. "It's an exposé of Hollywood, seen through your eyes. It's defiance of the shitty system that hangs you out to dry."

"Paige…" Avalon got up and walked offstage, behind the curtains.

With that one word, Paige's spirits plummeted. She'd upset her and probably embarrassed her. An ache rose inside, pounding against her stomach and spreading to her chest. She held a finger up to Dee Jae and followed Avalon.

Paige found her behind the curtain, standing there with her head down.

"Avalon, I'm so sorry, I didn't mean to—"

She held up the script. "Is this how you see me?"

"It's how I see the industry. And you're a product of that industry, someone who didn't deserve to be blackballed."

"It reads like a self-inflicted gunshot wound."

"It's meant to be a platform for all the crazy things that happen and all the things you wish you could say."

"You've taken the stories I told you and turned them into a circus, Paige. The assistant that got fired over the dead goldfish, the chair that got thrown out the window, the kitty-litter piss box…these are real stories."

"And they show how celebrities can be enabled by their handlers to such a severe degree that they begin to act insane. Actors are allowed, even encouraged sometimes, to go to such extremes that they become almost expected. And then, when the backlash hits, you're the ones that go down—not the managers, the agents, the producers, or the directors. How many stars have died of drug overdoses because everyone in their lives said yes to anything they wanted?"

"But the worse part is that you detail my…my downfall like it's a Saturday-morning cartoon."

"In some ways it has been."

Avalon turned to leave and Paige grabbed her by the arm. "I'm not saying your life is a cartoon. I'm saying your life has been made into a cartoon. One you never asked for."

"This just underscores what I'm trying to distance myself from, don't you see?"

"It separates you from it, Avalon. This play allows you to disconnect from the hype and show that it's a role you play, just like the ones in front of the film cameras. You get to stand up and call out this thing that's called Hollywood. You get to tell it like it is, bare bones and naked ass, and rail against the part of this business that is bullshit."

Avalon pushed the script toward her. "This turns my life into a folly."

Paige took it. "Did you read the last few pages?"

She shook her head, and Paige realized she was on the verge of angry tears.

"The set is Hollywood Boulevard. You walk upstage and stop. In a lone spotlight, you begin to speak." Paige opened the script to the second-to-last page and looked at Avalon, whose expression had turned hard. She took a deep breath and began to read the last part of the monologue. "Puppets? Yes. Actors go by many names. We are puppets, dummies, patsies, flunkies, and meat on a stick. Alfred Hitchcock's words still hold unbearable truth today, 'I never said all actors are cattle; what I said was all actors should be treated like cattle.'

"And how about you paparazzi? The ones who make a living off our lives? You chase us down for years and years, like hounds after the scent of blood. You think nothing of cashing in on the worst of our lives. The predator in you isn't interested in the good we do, in the charity we perform. You're in it for the money.

"The same stands for many directors and producers. You love riding the wave with us, but you're also comforted by the fact that when we crash and burn, the next starlet will be there. You step over us when we go down in flames.

"And down we go.

"All for the sake of art.

"Is it?

"I admit I have caused my own hype. I'm solely responsible and have let you feed off the spoils. I lost the distinction between the role I play on film and that which is my real life. And yet, I have always separated the two, working competently and professionally in the jobs that I have been given.

"But I'm sure, unlike me, that you paparazzi, directors, and producers could stand the scrutiny of a microscope aimed at your personal lives. I mean, you never argue with your girlfriend or get falling-down drunk. Of course not. You must certainly never say the wrong thing to anyone.

"And yet, I do. I have. And you've been there to get it all on film or have been ready to make the phone call of rejection.

"The line between my work and my life becomes blurred to everyone. Even me. The buzz starts, the blemished images become reality, and then the jobs fizzle. No one remembers the work you do because there are too many pictures of the dirty laundry left hanging out to dry.

"But the work is what I live for. A well-known saying in this town is 'Everyone adores you when you're dead.' They all quickly jump on board and become a fan. When I die, don't jump on my death wagon. Say what you will while I'm still here. And I'll do the same."

When Paige finished, she paused as a bubble of nervousness caught in her throat from the frank and undisguised words she'd written. She gave Avalon a moment to absorb it all and then looked up to meet her eyes.

"Is this what you believe?"

"I do. And it's what I hope you believe, too."

Avalon's look was intense. Her eyes bored into Paige's and seemed to be deep in contemplation. Would she be hurt and angry? Were Paige's words too offensive or revealing?

Finally, she drew Paige close, enfolding her in her arms. "I do."

She kissed her for the first time since that day at the Chateau Marmont. Her lips were soft and so inviting. For a moment, Paige was not backstage or really anywhere other than with Avalon. Her touch and taste and feel were her only sensations, and her heartbeat quickened.

This was where she wanted to be. No matter what the press said or the producers did, Avalon was a beautiful woman inside and out.

"I've missed you," Paige said. "So much."

"Me, too, baby. I'm so sorry."

They kissed again and Paige said, "Are you interested in doing the play?"

"Hell, yes."

A whoop of joy rose from the other side of the curtain.

Paige laughed. "You just made Dee Jae happy."

"I want to make you happy."

A deluge of relief gushed through Paige's body, dousing her previous nervousness into oblivion. She took Avalon's hand. "I'd say that's a plan."

Chapter Twenty

Michele D. looked confused when she arrived at Dee Jae's theater. Avalon's entire body crackled with energy as she met her out front and took her in. Billy was already there, and Avalon showed Michele D. to the seat next to him. The rest of the 150-seat theater was full and the buzz of low-level conversations filled the room. The stage curtain was down and soft jazz played from the overhead sound system.

"What's going on, Avalon?" Michele D. said, unable to sit down completely in her seat. "We're supposed to have our meeting with Garrett Chain right now!"

"We are," she said, and nodded over Michele D.'s head.

Both Michele D. and Billy turned around. Garrett Chain was sitting a few rows back, looking equally perplexed. Michele turned back around and sunk into her seat.

Seeming exasperated, she mouthed, "What the fuck?!"

"I called his office and changed the meeting location. See you in a few," Avalon said, and left them to join the rest of the cast and crew backstage.

Paige was there and Avalon hugged her, more from happiness than from anxious nerves.

"Are you all right?" Paige said.

"I'm great. I've got nothing to lose, actually." She kissed her. "Not now, anyway."

Dee Jae addressed the huddle of actors and playwrights. "I'm very proud of all of you. Tonight we have fun. Go out there and enjoy yourselves!" She made her way to the stage and Paige and Avalon watched from the wings.

"Ladies and gentlemen," Dee Jae said to the audience. "Thank you for coming to our showcase. We are very pleased to present to you our night of one-act plays. Our first, from writer Paige Cornish, is *Underneath It All*." She raised her arm, level to her waist, bowed slightly, and walked off the stage as the curtain rose.

The entire backdrop was an enormous, life-size painting of Sunset Boulevard, on the corner of Vine Street, looking west. The 1960s geodesic icon of the Cinerama Dome was in the background and the boulevard was busy with the blur of traffic.

"Break a leg," Paige said as Avalon walked on to the stage.

Dressed in a shimmering silver knee-length dress, she looked radiant and sophisticated. Paige held her breath and bunched up her fists, trying to quell her nervousness.

Avalon began her monologue. Of the one-act plays that night, hers was the only one-woman piece. And it seemed appropriate that Dee Jae had started with it because it was a real-world soliloquy that would herald the fictional pieces that followed.

As she spoke, Paige watched her own words become wholly Avalon's. This was a declaration of Avalon's Hollywood, a simple but direct discourse about the experience of one actor and the frank disclosures not many were bold enough to express. In the weeks since Avalon had been blackballed, her agent and manager had imposed a compulsory exile that had silenced her thoughts and feelings. This stage finally provided the platform for her voice to be heard. Good or bad, Avalon was in it now, moving with her words, striding across the stage, looking out into the audience and asserting herself.

Avalon had pointed Garrett Chain out to her and she watched him for a reaction. His face was as frozen and immobile as an icy lake. When Avalon got to the last part of her monologue, Garrett cocked his head to the side like a German shepherd reacting to a shrill whistle.

"But the work is what I live for." Avalon had come back to center stage to stand in a lone spotlight. "The work is what I want to be remembered by. A well-known saying in this town is 'Everyone adores you when you're dead.' They all quickly jump on board and become a fan. When I die, don't jump on my death wagon." She paused and her chest rose as she inhaled deeply, proudly. "Say what you will while I'm still here. And I'll do the same."

Paige jumped when the audience erupted in applause. Avalon still had a serious look on her face, but she could read the triumph in her body language as she walked off the stage and into the wings. They grabbed each other, hugging tightly as Dee Jae clapped Avalon on the back.

"Fantastic!" she said as she went back onstage to announce the next act.

Avalon felt glorious. The monologue had been more therapeutic than she'd imagined. From the wings, she looked out into the audience.

"Oh, no," Avalon said.

Garrett Chain had gotten up and filtered through the row toward the exit aisle.

Michele D. and Billy saw him leave, as well, and their pale complexions predicted the temperament of the conversation that awaited her.

Avalon and Paige had been backstage no more than five minutes when Michele D. and Billy found them in the green room.

Michele D. skipped the formalities of a greeting. "Are you fucking kidding me?"

The few actors and writers who were there exited quickly, and the room suddenly felt both cavernous and confined.

Girding herself for what had already transpired and was now inexpugnable, Avalon said, "It's done, Michele. I needed to say what I said."

"Did you *need* to commit professional suicide? What the hell were you thinking? And inviting Garrett Chain here? Are you fucking—" Aggravation rose so quickly that she stopped speaking.

Billy took his turn. "I'll call him and apologize. Or tell him it was meant to be a farce."

"It wasn't a farce." A wisp of dread curled up Avalon's spine. "I'm an actress and I performed a monologue. It was what I wanted to do, and you're not going to call and apologize or lie about it."

Michele D. threw her head back like an abandoned marionette and looked at the ceiling. "Jesus."

Avalon took Paige's hand and said, "We're going to enjoy the rest of the showcase, so if you don't mind…"

As they walked out, Paige squeezed her hand. "Are you okay?"

"I hope so."

❖

The marine layer was dense that night, choking the moon from its connection with Earth. Because of that, the ocean below Avalon's house was indistinguishable from the sky. Only the recurrent swell of waves rumbling their approach and crashing on the sand gave any indication of its existence.

Paige had Avalon in her arms and they lay in bed under the comforter. She brushed a lock of hair from her cheek and felt the full and wonderful weight of her lover when she inhaled and sighed deeply. "You seemed a little distracted when we made love. I can only imagine tonight was intense."

Avalon sighed again. "I'm not sure what the fallout will be from the play. The audience seemed to love it, and there will probably be a review about it tomorrow. But movies about movies don't usually do well."

"Because producers and directors hate for their inner sanctum to be exposed?"

"Exactly. And I frickin' did some pretty good exposing."

"Do you regret doing it now?"

"No. Not at all. There are a lot of things I regret, but not tonight."

"But you're worried about making matters worse?"

"Yeah. I keep telling myself to stick to my guns and not panic."

"Remember RSUA," Paige said.

Avalon turned in Paige's arms and looked at her. "Are you—"

"Don't interrupt the teacher. Now, follow me. Take slow, deep breaths in and out. Four times."

Avalon laughed.

"That's not breathing."

She settled back in Paige's arms and they breathed together, slowly and deeply. After four cycles, they lay together quietly, listening to the cadence of the ocean's surges.

Avalon broke the silence. "I adore you."

Paige kissed her cheek, inhaling the lovely scent that was exclusively Avalon. The light, floral aroma reminded Paige of forsythias, which seemed so perfect because that very flower comes to life after a long, harsh winter and bursts into colors overnight.

"I'm so proud of you."

"At my last AA meeting, I realized something. A person there was speaking about how our brains can talk us into anything, how they can make us believe whatever we want or convince us to chase certain needs. I thought of my work and the never-ending circus that follows, and then I understood the difference between what my head wants and what my heart wants. I'd lost the ability to separate the two. I thought what my head wanted was exactly what my heart wanted. I was convinced that all the things my brain said—*you need your fans, you have to stay in the limelight*—was all that mattered."

She raised up and faced Paige. "I couldn't see past my head and was doing such stupid things. My heart was nowhere in the mix. Then I realized that's where you live. So as I sat there at the meeting, a clear-cut equation came to me." She pointed as she said, "Head equals celebrity and heart equals…you."

It was that simple, Paige thought. A million details could blur the picture, but Avalon's simple math made sense.

"I love you, Avalon Randolph."

Before kissing her again, Avalon said, "I love you, Paige Cornish."

❖

The morning sun was shooing the beach fog from the coast. Avalon and Paige sat across the street from the house, at the edge of the bluff overlooking the ocean. Their cups of coffee sat on either side of them on a memorial bench dedicated to the early 1900s film director Thomas Ince. They had a bag of bread slices and were throwing them in the air for the seagulls that crisscrossed above them, squawking noisily as they snatched pieces in midair.

"I'm still deliriously happy from the reviews of *Underneath it All*," Paige said.

"Who knew that practically everyone in town would be praising your play?"

"It's mind-blowing."

"I've been thinking," Avalon said. "I'd like to find some land and design my first home. Of course I'd need an architect, but I want to create something amazing."

"That sounds wonderful." Paige moved closer and kissed her.

"Who knows? Maybe I'll go to college and study architecture so I can design it myself."

"I think that would make you happy."

"Being with you makes me happy, Paige."

At that moment, Avalon looked so humble and hopeful that being with her was natural and easy.

A horn honked and they turned to see Michele D.'s car coming down the street. It pulled into her driveway, and Michele and Billy jumped out and trotted up to her door. Avalon shouted and waved them over. It was incredibly comical to see Michele D. trying to run in a designer dress. Behind her, unathletic Billy, in his black business suit, looked like a mortician chasing a runaway casket.

"Avalon!" Michele reached them and paused, her mouth open as she sucked in whatever air she'd lost in the past eighty feet. "Garrett called this morning."

Paige instinctively reached for Avalon's hand. She didn't know which direction the news would take, but she wanted Avalon to know she was right there.

"And?" Avalon said.

"You're in."

"In?"

"Yes! He was impressed by the play. He thought it was an unusual place for a meeting and commented that it was rather one-sided, but he understood your message. Lord knows, I crapped fifteen pounds because of it."

Billy was huffing and puffing, too. "We just drove straight from his office. The same agreements and conditions came back on the table and we inked the deal!"

Avalon jumped up. "Are you serious?"

Michele D. put her hand to her chest. "As the heart attack I'm about to have."

Avalon let out a whoop and Paige jumped up to hug her.

"Money for college!" she said to Paige, who laughed.

Michele D. cocked her head. "What?"

"Nothing." She hugged Michele and Billy. "This is great news!"

"It sure is! And we're going back to our offices to get the word out," Billy said. "Lots of stuff to do. Interviews, news stories, blogs."

As they walked back to their car, Avalon called out, "Think we should take Paige's play on the road?"

Without turning around, they both shouted at the same time, "NO!"

"So," Avalon said when Michele D. and Billy had driven away, "I'll be heading to Spain eventually, but not before I go with you on your book tour."

"You want to go?!"

"I sure do. Who else is going to help you perfect RSUA technique?" Avalon said.

"Relax, stop negative talk…ahhh…"

"Use coping statements and acknowledge your feelings. See? You've forgotten already."

"I didn't, actually. I wanted you to feel needed."

Avalon hugged her. "I already do."

Paige sighed. "So, Spain, huh?"

"Is your passport up to date? I'm sure there will be some photo safaris for you to go on."

"It sure is."

"Good, because this film is going to be great! It's a huge blockbuster love story. Top billing."

"It's funny how your business works. You killed your costar in the last film and the next one will be a happily-ever-after."

Avalon draped her arms over Paige's shoulders. "That'd be a great name for your next book."

Paige moved closer, wanting to kiss her again and again. "Let's just keep that one for ourselves."

About the Author

Lisa Girolami (LisaGirolami.com) has been in the entertainment industry since 1979. She holds a BA in fine art and an MS in psychology and is a licensed MFT specializing in LGBT clients. Previous jobs included ten years as a production executive in the motion picture industry and another two decades producing and designing theme parks for Walt Disney and Universal Studios. She is now a Director and Senior Producer with Walt Disney Imagineering.

Writing has been a passion for her since she wrote and illustrated her first comic books at the restless age of six. Her imagination usually gets the best of her and plotting her next novel during boring corporate meetings keeps her from going stir crazy. She currently lives in Long Beach, California.

Books Available From Bold Strokes Books

Cut to the Chase by Lisa Girolami. Careful and methodical author Paige Cornish falls for brash and wild Hollywood actress Avalon Randolph, but can these opposites find a happy middle ground in a town that never lives in the middle? (978-1-60282-783-7)

More Than Friends by Erin Dutton. Evelyn Fisher thinks she has the perfect role model for a long-term relationship, until her best friends, Kendall and Melanie, split up and all three women must reevaluate their lives and their relationships. (978-1-60282-784-4)

Every Second Counts by D. Jackson Leigh. Every second counts in Bridgette LeRoy's desperate mission to protect her heart and stop Marc Ryder's suicidal return to riding rodeo bulls. (978-1-60282-785-1)

Dirty Money by Ashley Bartlett. Vivian Cooper and Reese DiGiovanni just found out that falling in love is hard. It's even harder when you're running for your life. (978-1-60282-786-8)

Sea Glass Inn by Karis Walsh. When Melinda Andrews commissions a series of mosaics by Pamela Whitford for her new inn, she doesn't expect to be more captivated by the artist than by the paintings. (978-1-60282-771-4)

The Awakening: A Sisterhood of Spirits novel by Yvonne Heidt. Sunny Skye has interacted with spirits her entire life, but when she runs into Officer Jordan Lawson during a ghost investigation, she discovers more than just facts in a missing girl's cold case file. (978-1-60282-772-1)

Murphy's Law by Yolanda Wallace. No matter how high you climb, you can't escape your past. (978-1-60282-773-8)

Blacker Than Blue by Rebekah Weatherspoon. Threatened with losing her first love to a powerful demon, vampire Cleo Jones is willing to break the ultimate law of the undead to rebuild the family she has lost. (978-1-60282-774-5)

Another 365 Days by KE Payne. Clemmie Atkins is back, and her life is more complicated than ever! Still madly in love with her girlfriend, Clemmie suddenly finds her life turned upside down with distractions, confessions, and the return of a familiar face... (978-1-60282-775-2)

Silver Collar by Gill McKnight. Werewolf Luc Garoul is outlawed and out of control, but can her family track her down before a sinister predator gets there first? Fourth in the Garoul series. (978-1-60282-764-6)

The Dragon Tree Legacy by Ali Vali. For Aubrey Tarver time hasn't dulled the pain of losing her first love Wiley Gremillion, but she has to set that aside when her choices put her life and her family's lives in real danger. (978-1-60282-765-3)

The Midnight Room by Ronica Black. After a chance encounter with the mysterious and brooding Lillian Gray in the "midnight room" of The Griffin, a local lesbian bar, confident and gorgeous Audrey McCarthy learns that her bad-girl behavior isn't bulletproof. (978-1-60282-766-0)

Dirty Sex by Ashley Bartlett. Vivian Cooper and twins Reese and Ryan DiGiovanni stole a lot of money and the guy they took it from wants it back. Like now. (978-1-60282-767-7)

The Storm by Shelley Thrasher. Rural East Texas. 1918. War-weary Jaq Bergeron and marriage-scarred musician Molly Russell try to salvage love from the devastation of the war abroad and natural disasters at home. (978-1-60282-780-6)

Crossroads by Radclyffe. Dr. Hollis Monroe specializes in short-term relationships but when she meets pregnant mother-to-be Annie Colfax, fate brings them together at a crossroads that will change their lives forever. (978-1-60282-756-1)